"I don't see the car that was following us," Selena said.

She turned back around in her seat. "I think you lost him."

"Not for long." Nicholas drove down the side street a second time. "We're going hunting. I want to know who is so interested in us."

Selena nodded. "Good. We need answers."

He chuckled. "We?"

"Yes, you said we would work together on the case that might clear my cousin's name. Or do you want me to do it alone? I will if I have to."

* * *

CAPITOL K-9 UNIT:
These lawmen solve the toughest cases
with the help of their brave canine partners

Margaret Daley, an award-winning author of ninety books (five million sold worldwide), has been married for over forty years and is a firm believer in romance and love. When she isn't traveling, she's writing love stories, often with a suspense thread, and corralling her three cats that think they rule her household. To find out more about Margaret, visit her website at margaretdaley.com.

Visit the Author Profile page at Harlequin.com for more titles.

SECURITY
BREACH

MARGARET DALEY

HARLEQUIN® LOVE INSPIRED® SUSPENSE

Special thanks and acknowledgment are given to Margaret Daley
for her contribution to the Capitol K-9 Unit miniseries.

Recycling programs
for this product may
not exist in your area.

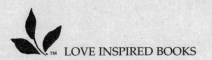

™ LOVE INSPIRED BOOKS

ISBN-13: 978-0-373-67683-5

Security Breach

Copyright © 2015 by Harlequin Books S.A.

www.Harlequin.com

Printed in U.S.A.

By whom also we have access by faith into this grace
wherein we stand, and rejoice in hope of the glory of God.
—Romans 5:2

To the brave men and women who are K-9 officers
and their canine partners

ONE

Nicholas Cole hurried toward the White House special in-house security chief's office in the West Wing, gripping the leash for his K-9 partner, Max. Two Secret Service agents emerged from the office, wearing gloves and carrying a folder. Both nodded toward him as he entered the room.

General Margaret Meyer stood behind her oak desk, her hands fisted on the tan blotter, a fierce expression on her face, her intense blue eyes narrowing on him. He swallowed hard. He rarely saw her this upset, but tension poured off her.

"Shut the door, Nicholas." The general moved from behind her desk, gesturing toward its flat surface. "This office has been searched."

After following her instruction, he came to attention in front of his boss, having a hard time shaking his military training in the Navy SEALs. "What happened?" He scanned the neat desk and the bookcase to the right, and wondered how she knew.

She straightened to her full height of five feet three inches, her shoulders thrust back. "When I went to get a folder from the bottom left-hand drawer, the stack was out of order. I have a very precise way of arranging everything in here, and thankfully I do or I might not have known someone went through the Michael Jeffries file."

The Jeffries case was an investigation being undertaken by the Capitol K-9 Unit, comprising fourteen cops, soldiers and special agents who looked into important cases and reported to Margaret Meyer, a former four-star general who worked under the president's direction. "Anything missing?"

"No, but it would be easy to take pictures of the papers and evidence the team has uncovered so far."

"What do you want me to do, ma'am?" Nicholas knew the murder of Michael Jeffries—son of the prominent congressman Harland Jeffries, who had been wounded in the attack against Michael—was important to the general, as well as to his unit captain, Gavin McCord. He and the rest of the team had pledged to find who killed Michael and left his father to bleed to death.

"Coordinate with Special Agent Dan Calvert who just left. You're to work with him on this. I want to know who was in my office. It could be the break we've needed on this case. I have Congressman Jeffries breathing down my neck. He wants answers to who killed his son. Not to mention Senator Eagleton insisting his daughter had nothing to do with Michael Jeffries's murder. Those two men have never been friends, and each one has a great deal of political clout."

Erin Eagleton, who'd been Michael Jeffries's girlfriend, was a person of interest in Michael's murder and the shooting of the congressman. Her starfish charm, with her initials engraved on it, had been found at the crime scene. Considering that Capitol K-9 Unit member Chase Zachary had run into Erin only hours before the murder and she'd been wearing the charm, the team desperately wanted to find Erin to bring her in for questioning. They'd been searching for her since Michael's murder. "I noticed Dan carrying a file from your office. Is he processing it for latent prints?"

"Yes, and any other physical evidence he can get. With the Easter Egg Roll today, the White House has been crawling with visitors since early this morning. Dan is going to view the security tapes and no doubt come up with a long list of suspects who had access." She shook her head, a scowl wrinkling her forehead. "Especially with the Oval Office and the Situation Room here in the West Wing being used for the festivities."

A security nightmare in his opinion, but the Easter Egg Roll was a long White House tradition. "When was the last time you opened that drawer?"

"Yesterday evening before I left for a reception in the Roosevelt Room then attended a state dinner for dignitaries from the UN. After that, I went home. I didn't come back here."

"Then we're looking at a sixteen-hour window."

General Meyer adjusted her horn-rimmed glasses. "So you see the problem. The list is much longer than I would like." She checked her wristwatch. "In fact, I need to put in an appearance at the Easter Egg Roll. I know the event is covered by the Secret Service, but I want you out there with Max. My office was breached and the perpetrator could likely be among the guests outside."

"May I inspect your office first?"

She nodded once. "I'll see you later. If you discover anything, find me right away. I want to be kept informed on everything."

"Yes, ma'am."

After the door closed, and he and Max were alone in the office, he unfastened the leash to his rottweiler and let him investigate. In addition to his usual duties as a guard/suspect-apprehension dog, Max was cross-trained on bomb detection, as an extra security precaution due to their post at the White House.

While Max moved around the room, Nicholas snapped on latex gloves and crouched behind the desk on the left side. He inspected the bottom drawer, then slid his hand back as far as he could under the piece of furniture, feeling for anything that might have fallen and rolled beneath it. Nothing.

Next, he examined a cabinet behind the desk. Underneath, his fingers touched something small. A cufflink? He pulled it out and scrutinized the gold cufflink with a bald-eagle imprint and the initials *VG*. How long had this been there? Did it belong to a visitor or the intruder?

After putting the piece of jewelry into an evidence bag and pocketing it, he continued his search of the office. Ten minutes later, other than the cufflink, he and Max had come up empty-handed.

"Time to go to the party, boy. General Meyer requires our attendance."

His rottweiler turned his amber-colored eyes on Nicholas and gave one bark.

Dressed in his black uniform with the emblem of the Capitol K-9 Unit on each sleeve and over his left pocket, Nicholas exited the West Wing by the West Colonnade and cut across the Rose Garden toward the South Lawn where the Easter Egg Roll was taking place.

For a few minutes he stood on the outskirts of the crowd assembled to enjoy the special party for the young children who'd won tickets by a lottery system. The kids were joined by various government officials, which included the president and his wife, and celebrities. The highlight was a visit by the Easter Bunny, but other costumed characters mingled among the crowd.

He scanned the people gathered, looking for anyone with the initials *VG*. His survey came to rest upon Selena Barrow, the White House tour director, responsible for planning this event. Even from a distance, Selena commanded a person's attention. Tall, slender with long wavy brown hair and the bluest eyes, she was attractive, but what drew him to Selena was her air of integrity and compassion. Since Erin had disappeared, Selena had been relentless in her support of her cousin's innocence, and he admired that kind of dedication.

When a couple with their two little girls stopped to talk to her, she smiled, bent down and spoke to the children. He glimpsed the radiant look on Selena's face. She probably was having as much fun as the kids at the event. Whenever he saw her with children, he got the feeling she must love being around them.

Last year he'd dated a woman who'd wanted

half a dozen kids. It hadn't taken him long to know they weren't a good fit. He didn't want to be a parent after the childhood he'd had. His father had certainly not been a good example to follow, and his mother hadn't been much better. He pushed thoughts of his past away and concentrated on the job he had to do today.

Selena would have an updated list of people invited to the party. It might save him a trip to the front gate if he asked her for it. And give him a reason to talk to her.

After slipping her keys back into her jacket pocket, her computer tablet nestled against the crook of her arm, Selena checked the schedule to see which age group of children would be doing the Easter Egg Roll next. Her friend Amy and her daughter were attending this year, and she wanted to cheer for Courtney in the egg roll.

Everything was set up. All the other activities were progressing according to plan—the Eggspress Yourself, the Eggtivity Zone Obstacle Course, the Rockin' Egg Roll Stage and the Storytime Stage with Senator Eagleton, her uncle, reading a Peter Cottontail book. A special appearance by the Easter Bunny would occur at the end of the story.

She watched her uncle entertaining the children sitting on the ground around him, his deep voice expressive, with the right inflection to convey the emotions of the characters. If only things had been different in her past, she and her uncle might have been on good terms. Instead, he barely acknowledged her because of her mother, his younger sister. He was polite but distant and reserved around Selena.

Selena wove her way through the crowd preparing to watch the Easter Egg Roll competition for the three-and four-year-old children. The president stepped into the fenced-off area to demonstrate what they were to do and start the race.

Selena pushed closer toward the activity. Moving quickly through the throng, Miss Chick, one of the costumed characters, bumped into her and nearly knocked Selena down.

Miss Chick, dressed in a feathered chicken outfit, steadied Selena and said, "Sorry. Late for the Eggspress Yourself," and scurried away, the daisy on her large straw hat swaying in the breeze.

Selena turned from watching Miss Chick disappear to continue toward the Easter Egg Roll and ran right into Nicholas Cole. Slowly she raised her gaze to his face, taking in his strong jawline, lips tilted in a grin, his deep brown eyes.

"Where are you going in such a hurry?" His

smoky voice with a slight Southern drawl always sent a thrill through her.

"The Egg Roll. To see if everything is going smoothly."

Being at least six inches taller than her five-nine, he scanned the mass of people who tried to get closer to the Easter Egg Roll. "From what I see everything is fine. You've done a good job."

"Thanks, but it isn't over with until this evening. I won't relax until then."

As if she could relax with her cousin missing. Since Erin's disappearance, Selena had constantly asked the Capitol K-9 Unit for updates about Erin's whereabouts, but she'd pestered this man the most because he was assigned to the White House. What was the Capitol K-9 Unit doing to find her cousin? To find the real killer of Michael Jeffries, Erin's boyfriend? There was no way she had murdered Michael. So far, Selena hadn't been successful in proving Erin was innocent, but she was getting closer. She'd been spending her off-hours investigating the cases Michael had been working on as an attorney. Maybe one of them was the reason he was killed.

"I have a favor to ask you." The dimples in his cheeks appeared.

And as usual she melted at the sight of them. He had the most engaging smile. "If I can help, I will." She didn't want to antagonize every member of the unit.

"I need a list of all the people attending today's events."

"All thirty thousand?"

"And the volunteers, too."

"Oh, what's an additional thousand or so. Security has that list."

Now, on top of the dimples, his brown eyes sparkled, luring her to forget she was working. "I know, but I thought you might have it on your tablet. It's important." He tapped the device she held in her hands.

"Only the volunteers. The full list is in my office." She glanced toward the West Wing and realized it was closer than Security. "I can pull it up on my computer for you."

"Please."

"I'd ask you why, but I'm sure you won't tell me for security reasons."

His grin grew.

Maybe if she did him a favor, he would return it and help her concerning Erin. "Let's go. Everything seems to be going fine. If not, I'm sure I'll be notified."

Nicholas looked toward General Margaret Meyer. "I need to tell the general something. Go ahead and pull the list up. I'll be right there."

As Selena headed toward the West Wing, she glanced at Nicholas talking to General Meyer.

The older woman frowned, clearly upset about whatever they were discussing. Did it have anything to do with Erin or the murder case? She knew her uncle, Erin's father, was insisting the general's team find the real killer.

Selena walked past the Rose Garden and entered the West Wing through the West Colonnade entrance. When she reached the door to her office, she slipped her hand into her jacket pocket for her keys. Nothing.

They were gone!

She just had them outside. She tried the knob, and it turned as though she'd never locked the door when she left hours ago. She always did. As she eased it open, it was wrenched from her grasp, and Miss Chick, in her yellow-feathered costume, latched onto her arm and dragged her into the office. Before she could react, Miss Chick smashed a vase against her skull. Selena fell backward, hitting the floor as Miss Chick fled.

She started to get up to alert Security, but the room spun before her. She sank back and closed her eyes. The darkness continued to swirl…

"Selena. Selena, are you okay?"

She pried her eyelids up and saw Nicholas's face looming close to hers. Worry lined his handsome features. A pounding in her head quickly reminded her of what had occurred. She tried to rise.

Nicholas clasped her shoulders. "Stay still. I've called Security and the doctor. Someone hit you with a vase." A latex glove on his hand, he held up a shard of a beautiful green-and-pink ceramic vase the president had given her when she'd first come to work as the White House tour director and his assistant.

"Do you remember what happened?"

"Did you see Miss Chick leave?"

Nicholas shook his head. The same costumed characters were hired every year for the event, and Nicholas had to be long used to seeing them all. "Does she have something to do with this?" He gestured to the mess in the office.

This time, despite the throbbing head, Selena propped herself up on her elbows and scanned the usually neat area. "She hit me with the vase and fled." Had she lost any consciousness? "How long did you talk with the general?"

"About five minutes then I came straight here." He spoke to Security through his invisible headset. "Miss Chick needs to be found and detained." He quickly described her costume. "She attacked Selena Barrow in her office."

Shortly, two security guards came into the room as well as Secret Service agent Dan Calvert. He took one look and said, "Fill me in."

Selena sat all the way up, trying to ignore the light-headedness swarming her. "I came to get the visitor list for Nicholas. That's when I discovered my keys were missing and the door was unlocked. The next thing I know, Miss Chick is grabbing me and yanking me inside then hitting me with a vase. She ran out after that. I don't know anything else."

"Your keys were stolen? Any idea when?" Nicholas asked, helping Selena to her feet and guiding her to a chair nearby.

She eased down, gripping the arms to steady herself. "I know exactly, but at the time I didn't realize it. Miss Chick bumped into me outside a few minutes before you and I talked. I had my keys until then."

Dan directed the security officers to stand guard outside the office. "What keys were taken?"

"To this office, my file cabinets, a storeroom around the corner and my house. I keep my car keys separate in my purse, which is locked in the top left drawer of my desk."

"Was that drawer key taken, too?"

"Yes."

Nicholas peered behind the desk. "Everything has been emptied." Donning a second glove, he moved toward the purse on the floor and held it up. "Check to see if anything was taken. We'll get to the bottom of this."

She took the brown Coach bag Erin had given her for her birthday. All her life Selena had fought for everything she had, so it was nice to have a champion for a moment, especially with all the tension of her cousin Erin named a person of interest in her boyfriend's murder and the shooting of Congressman Jeffries. That day, when they'd met to celebrate her birthday, her cousin had seemed so happy. Just a few weeks later, Michael was murdered…and Erin had disappeared.

Selena intended to help prove Erin couldn't have done it. Erin cared for Michael and wouldn't hurt anyone.

Then why did she disappear the night of the murder?

Selena refused to dwell on that nagging question and instead focused on what might be missing from her purse. She dumped the contents on her lap, her car keys falling out, and went through her wallet, then looked up. "No, everything is here."

The doctor arrived with his black bag. He quickly examined her, asking how she felt.

"My head hurts, but I'm all right. I've had worse headaches than this one." She couldn't leave the White House in the middle of the biggest affair she'd put together.

"Do you have any nausea?"

"No."

He checked the movement of her eyes, then the bump forming on the side of her head. "You'll have a knot, but there wasn't a cut, so no stitches. You should at least go to my office and let me do a more extensive evaluation in case you need to go to the hospital."

"I will later. I want to check and see if anything is missing from my office."

The doctor frowned but nodded. He looked toward Nicholas. "Make sure she does."

"I will."

The doctor turned back to Selena. "If you get dizzy or your vision is affected, blurry, bright-light sensitive, let me know immediately. Please rest as much as possible, and you can take over-the-counter pain meds for the headache. If it gets worse, let me know that immediately, too."

"I understand. If anything changes, I will."

When the doctor left, she swung her attention between Dan and Nicholas. "I want to see if anything has been taken, though Miss Chick didn't appear to have anything on her." Selena had to check a few files in particular to see if they were intact.

"If you're feeling up to it," Nicholas said, "Dan and I need to know that, too." Behind her desk, Nicholas bent over and picked up a straw hat with a daisy on it. "I'm assuming this isn't yours."

"No, it's Miss Chick's."

"Good. I'm going to use it to see if I can find where she went while Dan stays here with you."

Nicholas covered the distance to his K-9 partner, waiting near the door.

Taking hold of Max's leash, Nicholas showed the straw hat to the rottweiler, and the dog sniffed it. "Find, Max."

Nicholas and Max disappeared out into the hallway. Previously, when she'd seen Nicholas working with his K-9 partner, she'd always been amazed at Max's abilities. She hoped they'd find Miss Chick—whoever the costumed intruder really was.

Nicholas followed his dog through the crowds and out the door to the West Colonnade. Max headed east, stopping every once in a while and pointing his nose in the air, then charging forward. The dog entered the Rose Garden and headed to the lawn area bordered by flowering plants and boxwoods. The tulips were in full bloom, adding a brilliant splash among the greenery. Max came to a halt near the cluster of white furniture under a large magnolia tree and barked.

Nicholas checked the area, wondering if Miss Chick had sat here sometime recently. He moved behind two white chairs and inspected the bushes, plunging his hand into the middle. When he grasped a feathery material, glimpsing yellow, he tugged it free.

Miss Chick's costume—discarded.

"Good boy." He gave Max a treat.

He placed a call to Dan. "I found the costume in the Rose Garden minus Miss Chick. Are you still with Selena?"

"Yes. Do you want to talk to her?"

"Yes." When Selena came on, Nicholas asked, "Who's Miss Chick?"

"Just a minute. I'll have to look on my list of employees." A moment late, she answered, "Tara Wilkins."

"When she bumped into you earlier, could you tell if it was Tara Wilkins?"

A long pause—he could imagine her forehead creasing with a frown while her blue eyes darkened—then Selena said, "No, not for sure. Her voice was low and husky, but I'm pretty sure it was a woman."

"When was the last time you saw Tara Wilkins without the headpiece on?"

"When I talked with the costumed characters in the East Wing entrance before the event started. That was seven this morning."

"What do you know about Tara Wilkins? Is she trustworthy? Could she have given the costume to someone so the person could break into your office after the morning briefing?"

"She was Miss Chick last year and did a good job. The Secret Service vetted her as they do for all the people I use as costumed characters for this event, but I suppose it's possible."

"I'll have the police check her residence." He didn't have a good feeling about this.

"I don't see her putting her reputation on the line like that." Selena's worry came through the line.

"One good thing is that all the people who are here are on a list. You don't get in here without going through checkpoints."

"Please let me know what's happening. I'm responsible for the employees I hired for this event."

"I will. Anything missing from your office?"

"No."

"Let me talk with Dan again."

When Dan came back on the phone, he said, "I'll let Security know what's developing."

"Tara Wilkins needs to be found. Her residence checked. We don't have any idea what's going on. I'm not even sure it was Tara Wilkins in the costume, but I'm going to see if Max can follow the scent from the clothing. I'll let you know what I find."

"Good. In the meantime, I'm escorting Miss Barrow to the doctor's office."

Nicholas heard a protest coming from the background, and he smiled. Dan was going to have his hands full getting her to go. "Have fun. I'll check in later."

"Chicken," Dan whispered. "You left me with the toughest job. Anyone can follow a dog around."

Nicholas chuckled and disconnected the call, then let Max smell the yellow feathery costume. "Find."

As Max sniffed the air, Nicholas couldn't get the sound of Selena's voice out of his mind. What he had seen of her around the White House only reinforced the image of a woman dedicated to doing a good job. Did she think she had failed at her job by hiring Tara Wilkins?

As Nicholas followed Max through several areas of the Easter Egg Roll, he scanned his surroundings, wondering if the person who had discarded Miss Chick's costume was still here. If so, Max would find her—or possibly him. He had a photo on his phone of the volunteer who was supposed to be Miss Chick. If she wasn't the one who ran into Selena, then where was she?

Passing the Storytime Stage, Max dodged around the adults and children attending and finally came to a stop at the entrance to the women's restroom on the west side of the lawn.

Was the person still inside?

Nicholas started to look for a female security officer, but before he could, his rottweiler sniffed the ground then the air and took off toward the nearby exit to the event. When Nicholas emerged onto West Executive Avenue, Max halted in the middle of the road then trotted toward E Street. Near the Souvenir Egg Pickup, his K-9 came to another stop then wandered around the area but never picked up the scent again.

"Sorry, boy." Nicholas petted his dog. "She must have gotten into a vehicle. At least we know how she left and an approximate time."

Could that woman also be the same one who had gone through General Meyer's office? The intruder couldn't have picked a better day, with thirty thousand visitors and over a thousand volunteers. He'd have to watch a lot of security tapes to see if he could pinpoint who had ransacked the general's office and who had stolen Selena's keys. And why her keys? To rob her? Nothing was missing from her office.

Was something else going on here involving Michael Jeffries's case? That could be the connection between what had happened in General Meyer's office and in Selena's. Selena was a first cousin to Erin Eagleton—a person of interest in Congressman Jeffries's shooting and the murder of his son. When the Capitol K-9 Unit had begun investigating, Selena had been questioned to determine if she had helped Erin Eagleton disappear. They couldn't find anything to indicate she had assisted her cousin. Yet.

Did someone think Selena knew something? Did she? Had she helped her cousin somehow?

He hoped not. He would hate to have to arrest her if he discovered she had.

Security had been breached with the two break-ins —likely by someone who had been at the White House before, possibly a frequent visitor or staff member. This probably wasn't a spur-of-the-moment theft, and he would have to let General Meyer know about this latest development just as soon as he spoke to Selena again.

Max barked, interrupting Nicholas's thoughts.

"Come on, boy. Back to the party." Nicholas shortened the leash as they headed to the White House to find Selena.

A voice came over Nicholas's earbud. "We've found Tara Wilkins."

With Selena's keys in her possession? Or, had someone hurt Tara and taken the costume?

TWO

"Where is Wilkins? Is she all right?" Nicholas asked Security as he neared the White House.

"She was found drugged in the ground-floor restroom of the West Wing. The last time she was seen was in the Situation Room where kids were playing video games. Someone must have caught her in the restroom, and then stuffed her into a stall. One of our Secret Service agents found her. She talked to Tara, but the woman doesn't know who grabbed her. She's with the doctor in an examination room."

"I'm on my way now."

"I let Agent Calvert know about Miss Wilkins. He's already at the medical office with Miss Barrow. He's going to talk with her."

"So am I," Nicholas said to the man who manned the communication in the security office at the White House.

"Since he's working with you on the break-in at General Meyer's office, I'd like him to be included on anything concerning Selena Barrow. There could be a connection between what happened in her office and General Meyer's."

"I agree." Nicholas ended the call and moved inside.

He entered the Diplomatic Reception Room on the ground floor of the main-residence part of the White House. With Max beside him, he crossed the oval-shaped room of pale blue and bright yellow dominating the decor. Over the mantel hung a portrait of George Washington.

The doctor's office was located next to the Map Room off the central hall. When Nicholas went inside, Dan stood near the entrance into the examination area, with Selena sitting in a chair in the reception room.

Nicholas immediately went to her and took the seat next to her. She looked tired and frazzled. He couldn't blame her. It wasn't even noon and a lot had occurred in a few hours. He took her hand. "Are you still okay? No slurred speech, double vision or stumbling." He glanced toward his friend then Selena.

"No. I'm fine. Just angry. Dan said I could talk to Tara when you two finish. She's here because of me. I need to make sure she'll be all right. I want to find out what happened to her. Who did this? In the White House?"

"I understand. I want to find out the same things." His gaze locked with hers. "And I will."

"I appreciate it." Her eyes slid closed for a few seconds before connecting with his again.

Rising, he gestured toward Selena and said to Max, "Sit. Stay." When Selena glanced from his K-9 to him, he added, "I thought he could keep you company."

She petted Max. "Thanks."

Before he could head into the exam room, Dan pulled him aside to a private area. "Security is concerned about the link to the break-in at Margaret Meyer's office, although I'm not sure what the connection would be."

"It could be the Michael Jeffries case. Erin Eagleton is Selena's cousin. Maybe someone thinks she knows where Erin is. My unit has speculated she might know."

"Maybe Selena is someone you should get to know better." Dan winked.

"Yeah, sure, because Selena will take me to see the cousin she's hiding. If she does know where Erin Eagleton is, do you think she'd let it slip? Selena is sharp. Anyone who can coordinate this event and retain her sanity has to be."

"Personally, I wish they'd drop the tradition. It would make my life as a Secret Service agent tasked with keeping the president safe much easier. I get nervous with so many strangers around here."

Nicholas slapped Dan on the back. "Your life

is easy. You usually stand around watching people go by. Not too strenuous, if you ask me."

"I didn't," Dan grumbled as they walked back over to the exam room. He rapped on the door before they entered.

The nurse left as Dan introduced Nicholas to Ms. Wilkins. "I know you can't remember much, but he has a few questions concerning what happened to you."

"I could use your help, Ms. Wilkins. The person who drugged you and took the Miss Chick costume deliberately bumped into the White House tour director to steal her keys, so anything you can tell me will help me find the perpetrator. Please describe what happened and where you were."

The young woman scrunched her forehead and stared down at her hands. "Everything is hazy. I remember leaving the Situation Room and going to the restroom. I was the only one inside. I was surprised because so many people were attending the event, but while I was in the stall, I heard the door opening and someone coming in." Closing her eyes, she lowered her head for a few seconds. "The last thing I recollect is leaving the stall, a sound behind me, then a prick at my neck. Nothing after that until I was found."

"Anything about the person who drugged you. A glimpse? A scent?"

She massaged her temples then shook her head. "My mind is foggy. I…"

"How tall are you?"

"Five feet ten inches. Why?"

"It gives me an idea how tall the fake Miss Chick is." Nicholas removed his business card and handed it to her. "If you remember anything, even if you think it won't help, call me and let me know."

"I will, but I didn't see who it was."

Nicholas rose from the chair. "Thank you, Miss Wilkins. Miss Barrow is outside and wants to make sure you're all right."

"I feel so bad. This was a big gig for me."

"She's only concerned about your welfare." Nicholas left with Dan, and in the reception room motioned to Selena that she could talk with Tara Wilkins.

Selena passed him, giving him a small smile, but it didn't wipe the weariness from her expression. While Selena disappeared into the exam room, he waited out in the empty reception area with Max. Nicholas stared at the closed door.

"I told you Ms. Wilkins didn't know anything," Dan said, breaking the silence.

"I saw Miss Chick approach Selena, and from a distance it appeared the costume fit her well, so the assailant is about the same height. Selena thinks it was a female."

"Is she sure?"

"No, but that will be easy to find out. A male going into a woman's restroom will probably stand out on the security tapes."

"That area of the hallway won't be on tape. It's a dead end, but the hallways leading to it are on camera. So any male seen turning the corner could be going to the men's restroom. It's taken me years to learn every area that's covered and the ones not." Dan grinned. "And then the powers that be change things around."

Nicholas paced the room. "Oh, joy. You and I get to watch hours of tape, and we might come up with nothing."

Dan shrugged. "You know how investigations go. Most take a lot of legwork."

"I've contacted Security about changing the lock on Selena's office and storeroom. Did you check it to see if it was searched?"

"Yes, on the way here, but it didn't appear to have been."

"What did the doc say about Selena's injury?"

"The doctor checked her again and gave her instructions about what to watch for, but he thinks the concussion is a mild one."

"When this is over with, I'm escorting Selena home." Nicholas stopped in front of Dan. "I want to make sure everything is all right. With her head injury and the fact someone has her keys, I won't rest well if I don't see for myself that she'll be okay and safe at her house."

"And that's a great opportunity for you to get closer to her. I can see why you've been with her today. I still think she could lead you to her cousin. They're about the same age. They're related and friends. The things we do for an investi…" Dan's voice trailed off into silence, his eyes growing round as he stared behind Nicholas.

He swung around and found Selena glowering at them, her face pale, her hands trembling.

She charged across the office. "I need to get back to work."

"Wait up." Nicholas gripped Max's leash and hurried after her, the sound of Dan's chuckles irking him.

Selena kept going, her free hand fisted at her side.

Outside the ground-floor entrance, Nicholas caught up with her. "I'm sorry about what Dan said."

She whirled toward him, fire shooting out of her eyes, her jaw set in a fierce line. "Is it true? You've talked to me more in the past couple of months than the whole year before. You can tell your team I don't know where my cousin is, but Erin is innocent. She could be dead or kidnapped and all you think is she murdered her boyfriend. She cared for Michael and wouldn't have hurt him. She wouldn't have hurt anyone."

He let her storm away because what she'd said

had a ring of truth to it. He had started talking to her more because of the case. Although there was no evidence to support that she was helping her cousin, he and other members had to follow all leads. He'd learned in this profession to be distrusting and question everything. At this moment, as Selena vanished in the crowd near the Easter Egg Roll, he regretted that aspect of his job.

By the end of the event in the early evening, anger still roiled in Selena's stomach whenever she glimpsed Nicholas in the crowd or thought about him. She liked him—a lot—but overhearing him and Dan talking about her concerning Erin's disappearance, all the feelings she'd been fighting since her cousin went missing had surged to the foreground.

She'd caught a couple of Dan's earlier remarks—his voice a little louder than Nicholas's—before they'd gone in to see Tara Wilkins and then again later. She hated being the topic of conversation and especially the fact that the Capitol K-9 Unit had suspected her of assisting a fugitive—still did. Not that she wasn't trying to help Erin. She was. But by trying to prove she couldn't have killed Michael. If Selena could gather evidence her cousin hadn't shot anyone, then if Erin was alive and in hiding, she could return. But her greatest fear was that

Erin wasn't alive. All she knew—via the Capitol K-9 Unit—was that back in February, an elderly couple in rural Virginia had taken in an injured young woman matching Erin's description, but she'd left a few days later, her appearance dramatically altered. Weeks later, two thugs had terrorized the couple for information on Erin's whereabouts. Who were they? The killers? Bounty hunters?

And where was Erin? Reports had come in last month that someone in rural Virginia was using public computers to research bills introduced by Congressman Jeffries. Could that be Erin? If so, what was she looking for?

One angle Selena was following involved a case Michael Jeffries had been very passionate about. Michael had been working pro bono on a murder case for convicted killer Greg Littleton, a man who Michael believed was innocent. Perhaps the real killer wanted Michael off the case permanently and killed him. Maybe the killer had trailed Michael to his father's house, murdered him there, and when his father, the congressman, appeared, the killer shot him, too.

Lots of maybes and not a lot of answers. Selena hadn't had the time in the past few weeks to work on anything except the Easter Egg Roll, but she had managed to interview Greg Littleton in prison, convicted of murdering Saul Rather. Michael had been fervently working to prove

Littleton was innocent. Those who believed in his guilt weren't happy about that. As a crusading attorney, Michael had made himself some enemies.

Now that the Easter Egg Roll was over, Selena intended to devote more time to looking into the Littleton case and any others that appeared promising. Someone had killed Michael Jeffries and left his father for dead—and that someone wasn't Erin Eagleton.

As Selena approached her car in the staff's underground parking, she discovered Nicholas lounging against her white Ford Mustang with Max sitting next to him. How dare he look so innocent with those big brown eyes and cocky grin. He'd removed his ball cap and stuck it in his back pocket. His thick, dark blond hair was cut short but not military-style. Knowing his Navy SEALs background, that had surprised her when she'd first met him last year.

Her anger began to soften as she took in his casual stance, as though nothing was wrong. She quickly shored it up. She would not be used. Her mother had tried to get back in her big brother's graces by using Selena. It hadn't worked. Her uncle had recognized that his sister wasn't serious about not drinking, that all she needed his money for was to support her while she drowned herself in alcohol, leaving her daughter to fend for herself.

Selena had learned one thing growing up. She was the only one who would look out for herself. She ignored Nicholas as she unlocked her car and tossed her purse on the passenger seat.

"Max, what do you do when you're in hot water?" Nicholas said to his K-9.

The sound of the dog's bark echoed through the underground garage.

Selena pressed her lips together to keep from smiling. He was going to charm her. She'd seen him charming the women at the White House, and she wasn't going to buy into it. She'd watched her mother fall for one man after another, thinking he would take care of her.

But her current man had never stayed around long.

He tapped the side of his head with his palm. "Max, what a brilliant idea. I'll try that."

Nicholas sidled along the body of the car until he was half a foot from her right arm. The hairs on it tingled.

"I'm sorry. Nothing I did today had to do with your cousin. I was trying to point out to Dan the error of his suggestion with sarcasm."

Selena squeezed her eyes closed, her heartbeat accelerating at Nicholas's nearness. Finally she turned slowly toward him, backing away a step. "Be honest. Have you ever considered I might have been helping Erin stay hidden?"

"Honestly—yes. I'm not going to lie to you.

My team has looked into all the possibilities while searching for Erin, so being a friend and a family member, you would obviously be on that list. And if I was perfectly honest, at first that is why I initiated several conversations with you lately."

She tensed, flexing her hands. "I knew it. At least I appreciate your honesty. Now I need to leave. I'm tired, and I pray I don't fall asleep driving home."

"Then let me drive you to your house."

"I was trying to point out the extent of my exhaustion with exaggeration. I'm perfectly fine to drive myself. I'm not going to fall asleep at the wheel. In fact, with all that has been going on today, it may take hours for me to go to sleep."

He chuckled. "I know that feeling. My body is exhausted but my mind is racing a mile a minute."

She had to fight the urge to respond to his charm. Life lessons from her childhood taunted her. She would never be like her mother, depending on others, depending on alcohol to make it through the day. "This is not going to work." She stepped back again and encountered the open driver's door.

His expression sobered. "Seriously, I would like to escort you home. Someone took your house keys today. You should have your locks changed."

"Believe it or not, I've thought of that. I

know how to take care of myself. You should have seen the neighborhood I grew up in. The total opposite of Erin's childhood. My branch of the Eagleton family are the black sheep. I have a locksmith coming to my house in—" she checked her watch "—an hour. I need to be there so he can change my locks, so if you'll excuse me, I need to be going."

"Have it your way." Nicholas moved away from her white Mustang.

When she slipped behind the steering wheel, she inhaled a calming breath and started her car. As she backed out of the parking space, she noticed Nicholas open the rear door of an SUV only three vehicles away and wait for Max to jump into it. She went through the security checkpoint with Nicholas's black Tahoe a vehicle behind hers. When she turned right, he did, too. Her grip tightened as he continued to follow her.

Although she had nearly a full tank, she pulled into a gas station. Nicholas came up behind her.

She shoved open her door and marched back to his SUV. "What do you think you're doing?"

"Escorting you home the best way I can."

Her head pounding, she opened her mouth to give him a piece of her mind, but when she couldn't find the words she wanted to say, she snapped her teeth together, then spun on her heel and stalked to her Mustang. Fine. He could waste his time "escorting her home." That didn't mean she would talk to him or even acknowledge his presence.

As she continued her drive to her house in Arlington, she kept looking back to see if he was still behind her. Although it was too dark to see his face, she imagined his pleased expression for following through with what he'd wanted to do. There was one part of her that felt like a suspect being tailed and another part that warmed when she thought about him trying to protect her from the person who'd taken her keys—for what reason, she had no idea.

In college she'd had her purse snatched on campus when walking back to her dorm from the library late one night. She had been so angry she'd chased after the guy, caught up with him and tackled him to the ground. A campus cop who'd rushed to her aid had lectured her about the risk she'd taken. She supposed it had been foolish, but her reaction to being robbed was automatic. She'd come from a tough area of Washington, DC, and had learned to stand up for herself.

Selena pulled into her driveway and stared at her house, her first, earned by hard work after years of studying and being at the top of her class at school. She was going to prove to her uncle she wasn't like her mother and was willing to work for everything she got. She didn't want a free ride from him or anyone.

Her porch light illuminated the front part of her redbrick two-story home with white trim and green shutters. Hers—as of six months ago. She noticed Nicholas had parked at the curb and exited his Tahoe. He came around the hood. She quickly grabbed her purse, took a spare house key from the bottom of the driver's seat and climbed from her Mustang.

"That's as far as you need to go. You've escorted me home." She waved toward her house. "Nothing is amiss. You can run along now."

He planted his feet apart, crossed his arms and said, "Not until you go in the house to your front window and wave to me. Then I'll leave."

"What if I don't?" the imp inside her asked.

"Then I'll stay here all night."

His determined look drilled right through her. "You're impossible."

"It comes in handy when I deal with stubborn people."

"You think I know where Erin is."

"Do you?"

"No."

"Then I believe you."

"Really?"

"I told you I would be honest with you. I'm worried about you. I think something is going on. It might be connected to the Jeffries case or something else. I don't know. Miss Chick today went to some trouble to get your keys. Why?"

"To rob me?"

"There were a lot richer people there than you."

She lifted her shoulders in a shrug. "Maybe they thought I was wealthy since Senator Eagleton is my uncle. When you catch the person, ask her."

"I will. Nothing was taken from your purse in your office, so it wasn't that kind of robbery. Could the person have been after something—"

"I don't need a protector," she interrupted, remembering all the times she alone had protected herself from the predators in her childhood neighborhood. "I've been taking care of myself most of my life. Go home. Look out for yourself." Frustration churned her stomach.

"Just as soon as I know you're safe inside and the locksmith has arrived."

"Now you're putting more conditions on your leaving."

"What can I say? I changed my mind."

Clamping her lips together, she pivoted and strode toward her porch steps. As she mounted them, the feel of his gaze on her back made her shiver. For most of her life, she had been the only one who took care of herself. What would it be like to have someone who cared?

No! I won't go there. At times, she wasn't even

sure the Lord was there anymore. As a child she'd sought refuge in the local church, latching on to the promise that God loved her. But did He? While growing up, she'd been so alone.

Absorbed in thoughts of the past, she unlocked her front door and moved into the foyer. One look into the living room and she froze.

THREE

Selena stared at her trashed living room then, beyond at the dining room and part of her kitchen. What if the intruder was still here? She sidled toward the table nearby and pulled open a drawer. Keeping her eye on the staircase to the right, she felt for her revolver. When her fingers encountered the barrel, she quickly clasped the handle and withdrew it.

"What do you think you're going to do with that?" Nicholas's deep voice sounded from the entrance.

She glanced over her shoulder. "Defend myself. The person could still be in here."

"Put it on the table before someone gets hurt." Nicholas drew his gun.

"I know how to use it."

"I don't care."

She did as he ordered, actually relieved he was here. She must be more exhausted than she thought.

"Now, go outside, open my tailgate so I can call for Max, then you're to stay on the porch while Max and I search the rest of the house. If the locksmith comes, have him wait with you."

Selena nodded then headed to his Tahoe and released Max. She'd been around the rottweiler enough to know he was a well-trained dog. He could be fierce, but she wasn't afraid of him.

"Come," Nicholas said from the doorway.

Max trotted toward her house. Selena followed behind him and stopped at the top of the steps, gripping the post, trying to ignore her headache.

"Check it." Nicholas disappeared with Max into her house.

She lost sight of them when the pair went up the stairs. With only two bedrooms and a bath on the second floor, they were back in the living room within five minutes.

"Do you have a basement?"

"Yes. The stairs to it are next to the back door."

He and Max vanished around the corner into the kitchen. The whole time they were gone, her heartbeat thudded against her rib cage, her breathing shallow. What if the intruder was hiding in the basement? Or there was more than one person? When minutes later, Nicholas and Max rounded the corner and crossed the living room, she sagged against the wooden railing, not realizing until then how tense she'd been while they were checking out her house.

"Does the rest of my place look like the living room?"

"Yes. You'll need to go through your home and let me know what's missing. I'll contact the local police about what happened, but since this might be connected with the White House break-in, I want to deal with it."

"I'll do a walk-through tonight, but I'm too tired to do more than that." The past weeks finally wreaked their havoc on her.

"Why don't you wait until tomorrow. In fact, go to bed. I'll take care of the locksmith, dust for fingerprints since this is tied to a theft at the White House and stay until he leaves. Okay?"

She hesitated, so tempted by his offer.

"I'll make sure everything is locked up." Nicholas's gaze strayed to something beyond the porch.

She swung around and saw Mr. Lamb, the locksmith, park his van behind Nicholas's SUV. "I can't go to sleep until I know the locks have been changed. I want all three door locks replaced even though I only had the front one on the key ring."

"You might also think about getting an alarm system."

"Believe me, I will tomorrow."

After talking with the locksmith, Selena made

her way upstairs and changed into a pair of sweatpants, a large T-shirt and slippers. Her feet were screaming pain and demanding she sit, but she was afraid if she did, she would never get up, any surge of adrenaline she'd experienced from the break-in subsiding. After her locks were replaced, she would send Nicholas and Mr. Lamb on their way, do a brief walk-through to check if anything was missing, then collapse into bed with her revolver on the nightstand.

Selena's eyes popped open to a semidark room. A dull ache still gripping her head, she glanced at her digital clock on the bedside table: 7:00 a.m. She rolled over and tried to go back to sleep since the chief of staff had told her to take the next two days off. But after twenty minutes, she gave up.

Thoughts of what the intruder was looking for kept running through her mind. While Mr. Lamb changed the locks, she'd gone from room to room, checking if anything obvious had been stolen, but nothing was missing. Her computer was there but obviously had been handled by the intruder. She'd have it checked to see if something had been added or deleted. Her TV and a few pieces of nice jewelry had been untouched.

After seeing Nicholas out the door and locking it last night, she'd trudged up the stairs, and in spite of being totally drained emotionally and physically, she'd lain awake for another hour until exhaustion must have finally taken over.

Still dressed in her sweatpants and T-shirt, she finger combed her hair—because she didn't want to scare her neighbors—and headed downstairs to fetch her *Washington Post*. Her morning ritual always included savoring the newspaper with her coffee before she started her day. After she prepared the brew and it began to perk, she walked to the front door, opened it and nearly fell over Nicholas stretched out in a sleeping bag against the threshold to her home. She teetered over him.

He reached up and steadied her.

"What are you doing here?" She scanned the porch. "And where is Max?"

He rose, stretching and rolling his shoulders. "I'm making sure you're safe. Max is at the back door guarding that entrance."

"You didn't say anything about that last night. I saw you walk to your SUV."

"To get my sleeping bag." He grinned, a dimple appearing in his cheek. "I did leave your house, but I couldn't completely go. I would have never forgiven myself if the intruder had come back."

She marched past him and snatched up the newspaper at the bottom of the stairs, then retraced her steps. Planting herself in the doorway, she blocked him. "You didn't need to do that. I doubt the person would come back."

"Have you noticed anything missing?"

"That's what you really want to know. Admit it. That was the real reason you stayed."

"Only one of the reasons. I am concerned about your safety." He drew in a deep breath. "Ah, coffee. May I have some?"

She twisted her mouth into a frown, trying to be perturbed at the impossible man. But she couldn't. "One cup. Then you'll leave. I have a rare day off and want to…" What? Relax? Which had been her original plan until someone broke into her house. She glanced at her living room and knew that wouldn't happen until she cleaned it up. The only way she got everything done was to be highly organized; she wouldn't rest until this mess was taken care of.

"Could you use help putting this back the way it was?" Nicholas gestured toward the living room.

She opened her mouth to say no, then chuckled at how ridiculous that sounded. "My mama didn't raise no fool." Actually, her mother hardly raised her at all.

"I take that as a yes."

She nodded. "Come in."

Nicholas entered and shut the door. "I almost forgot. Mr. Lamb gave me the bill." He dug into his pocket and pulled it out. "I didn't want it to get lost in all this clutter."

She'd forgotten all about the bill last night. She'd been too focused on Nicholas prowling her house while Mr. Lamb worked. "Thank you. He would have sent it to me."

"You're welcome."

Pushing some clutter out of her way with her foot, she padded across the wooden floor to the kitchen and poured two mugs full of coffee. "Let's have it outside on the patio. I won't relax if I keep looking at all this. Besides, Max might want some water. There's a bowl on the counter. Use that to give him some."

"You're certainly a take-charge kind of woman."

At the back door, she peered at him. "It pays to be in my job since so much of it is planning various events for the president. He expects the best from his staff."

Nicholas filled the bowl with water. "Yesterday really showcased your talents. Everyone I saw was having a great time. Even Margaret Meyer. I don't think of her as having a sense of humor."

"Speaking of the general, won't she expect you at the White House this morning?"

Nicholas frowned. "I'll let her know I'll be in later. Dan can start looking at the security tapes."

"Dan is helping you with my case?"

"Yes."

"Why are you on it? I see Dan's role."

He averted his gaze for a long moment, then said, "Another office was broken into yesterday. There may be a connection."

Her face drained of color. "General Meyer's?"

He remained quiet.

"I heard there was a ruckus around her office. You know how rumors can fly around the White House. And you do work for her." Her eyes widened. "If you think there might be a connection, it has to be over the Jeffries case."

"No comment at this time."

She opened the door and stopped. Max, much like Nicholas, was lying down across the entrance into the kitchen.

Nicholas stepped over his rottweiler and put the bowl down on the patio. "Drink."

Selena watched Max saunter to the bowl and lap up the water. "You have to tell him to drink?"

"He waits for commands when we're on the job. When he's off duty, he does what he wants."

On the job? She guessed she was a job to him, especially if he thought she knew where Erin was. She tried to dismiss the thought but she couldn't. It hurt. "I wish I could get the people working under me that well trained," Selena finally said when she realized Nicholas was peering at her with that sharp, assessing look. Her heartbeat accelerated, and she sat in one of the chairs at the glass table.

"That's the result of months of training as well as continual refresher courses." Nicholas took the seat across from Selena.

"He's beautiful. I've never been around a rott-weiler until you came to the White House. Does he live at your place when you two aren't on duty?" She had to remember he was probably as distrusting as she was. Most people in law enforcement were.

"Yes. All the dogs in the Capitol K-9 Unit stay with their partners when off duty."

"I've never had a pet even as a child. And now I work all the time, so it wouldn't be fair to leave an animal alone so much."

"I had any pet I wanted."

There was a tone in his voice that indicated there was more to that statement than what he was saying. "So what did you have as a child?"

"A dog named Butch and a horse called Dynamite."

"So you rode, too?"

"Yes, I lived on a farm in Maryland growing up. I'd go riding whenever I could and Butch always followed."

His childhood was vastly different from hers. She'd grown up in Washington, DC, in the area that wasn't technically slums but close. "What did your family grow on the farm?"

"Nothing. They had some horses and that was about it."

"Some? How big was the farm?"

"Two hundred acres. In some people's book it was more an estate than a farm, although Thoroughbred horses were raised there."

"But not you?" Again she sensed an underlying tension in his voice and saw the stiffening of his shoulders.

"The house I grew up in was a mansion. A person could get lost in it. But to me it was only a place to sleep at night." A touch of bitterness laced his words.

Definitely a far cry from where she'd lived as a child. The biggest apartment she ever lived in was three rooms, if you counted a bathroom she could barely turn around in. "You didn't like your home?" she asked before she could snatch the question back. She had no business prying into his past. She told no one about hers.

"It wasn't a home. My family's business was a large import/export company. My parents were rarely there. Their work took them all over the world."

When her mother had been gone, it was because she was drinking and would disappear for days. "You never got to travel with them?"

"No." His mouth snapped closed, and he averted his face, staring at Max sniffing around the yard. "I noticed your flat-screen TV and laptop are still in the house, so what would some-one be looking for? Do you have any other valuables?"

"Not much. I've poured all my money into this house. I bought it last year and have slowly been fixing it up the way I want. It's the first place I've really called home." The words slipped out before she could stop them. She quickly added, "I lived in apartments while going to school and my first couple of years working in the White House," as though that would explain why she'd never felt at home anywhere before she'd bought this place.

"That's how I feel about my house in Burke. As a Navy SEAL I traveled a lot and lived on base, but now that I'm working for the Capitol K-9 Unit, I can put down some roots."

"Do you have to do much traveling? I know you come and go at the White House, but I figure you're working on a case."

"Although I'm assigned to the White House, I'm at headquarters for briefings, coordination with other team members, running down leads and training sessions with Max." Nicholas took a sip of his coffee, his gaze connecting with her over the rim of his mug.

"The locksmith changed my locks last night, so why did you and Max stay?"

"It was late when Mr. Lamb left. By the time

I went home, I'd probably only get a few hours' sleep before coming back here this morning."

"But you had to be uncomfortable on the porch."

"As an ex–Navy SEAL, I'm used to sleeping on the hard ground. I slept great because I was on your porch. If I'd left you, I'd have worried about you and probably not slept at all. It's traumatic for a person to discover her house was broken into. I wanted to make sure you were okay and whoever did this didn't come back. As I mentioned yesterday, I'd recommend getting a good alarm system today. Mr. Lamb put on sturdy locks, but they only go so far. Having a dog wouldn't be a bad idea, either."

She smiled. "Will you loan me Max?"

"Sorry, we're an inseparable team," he said with a chuckle. "But a dog like Max would be perfect."

Although she'd never had a pet, the idea interested her. "How would I get one trained and as well behaved as Max?"

"He's trained specifically for guarding, apprehending suspects and searching for bombs. You don't need that, but I can help you if you want."

"Let me think about it. I don't want to get a dog if I can't give him the attention he needs." If she accepted Nicholas's help, she would be spending a lot more time with him. That could be dangerous because she couldn't deny her attraction to him.

His dark brown eyes gleamed. "Not all pet owners feel that way. They buy an animal and then ignore it most of the time."

Selena downed the last of her coffee. She could get used to his presence; she needed to end this. "I appreciate your concern last night, but I think I'll be all right today. The break-in was a shock, but it takes a lot to rattle me, so on second thought, I don't need your help cleaning up." She rose. "I'll look into an alarm system since I'm off for a couple of days. But my main concern is righting my house and seeing if anything was stolen. At first glance, nothing is missing, but if that were the case, then why did someone risk breaking in?"

"Looking for something?" He pushed to his feet.

She frowned. "I don't keep anything related to my White House job here. That's why I often stay late at night. I try to leave my work at my office. When I come here, it's my downtime."

"Good way to be. I need to do that more myself."

She started for the back door. "It's probably harder because Max stays with you."

"That's not it. I've never been a person who can just relax and do nothing."

"So no vacations?"

"Not lately. Max and I have gone camping a few long weekends."

"I work hard, but I play hard, too. Maybe I could teach you how if you help me get the right dog." Here she went again. When was she going to learn? His help would come at a price.

"If you decide to have a pet, you've got yourself a deal. Are you sure about not needing any help cleaning up?"

"Yes, I'm sure you have work today. I hope you let me know if you find the person who drugged Tara Wilkins."

"I will." Nicholas turned toward Max. "Come."

His dog trotted to Nicholas's side, and they trailed her into the house. She was again greeted with the chaos, and dreaded the day before her. She released a long breath and realized the only way the cleanup would get done was to start and keep going until she was finished. She wouldn't go to bed tonight until she'd righted her house.

Selena walked with Nicholas and Max to the front door. "Thank you for your help yesterday at my office during the Easter Egg Roll."

He arched a brow. "So my help wasn't so bad, after all."

"Okay. I was a little miffed at you for thinking I'm harboring a suspect."

"A little? I'd hate to see your full-blown anger."

"It isn't a pretty sight, so that's a warning to stay on my good side," she said with a laugh.

"I'll remember that. Let me know if you're missing anything." He gave her a business card with his cell number on it. "Call if you have any trouble—" he cocked a smile "—or if you just want to talk."

"Just so you realize… If I can help my cousin, I will, but I don't know where she is. Erin didn't kill Michael.

He held up his hand before she could say anything else. "I'm leaving. I don't want to get into an argument about Erin's possible part in the murder."

As Nicholas strode away with Max at his side, Selena unclenched her hands, noticing the fingernail indentations in her palms. That man could certainly infuriate her…but also intrigue her. *Lord, give me the patience and guidance to help Erin. Open Nicholas's eyes to the truth.*

Nicholas spent the morning at Capitol K-9 Unit headquarters viewing security video from the morning that Selena was attacked. Next to him, Fiona Fargo, the team's tech wizard, studied video on hallways leading to General Meyer's office.

"Margaret Meyer is a busy lady," Fiona said, pushing her rolling chair away from her desk and twisting toward Nicholas. "This is a list of suspects who could have broken into her office and read the Jeffries case file during your time frame."

Nicholas stared at the fifteen names on the paper. "I want you to check into each one. Give me everything you can on them. Start with Vincent Geary—he's an aide to Congressman Jeffries. The initials on the cufflinks found in the general's office are *VG*. He's my top suspect at the moment. When I leave here, I'm going to pay Mr. Geary a visit."

"Do you want me to investigate General Meyer's secretary, too?"

"Yes, everyone who was in the office during those hours. We have to include everyone. If you find anything suspicious, let me know right away."

As Nicholas rose and stretched his stiff muscles, Fiona asked, "Where's Max?"

"In the training yard. I wanted to give him a little downtime. He's been working a lot lately." Nicholas walked toward the doorway of Fiona's office. "But his playtime is over."

"He's as driven as you are."

"You know how dogs and their owners are."

She shook her head. "Nope. I have cats."

"Don't let Max know."

Fiona smiled. "Oh, he knows. Why do you think he sniffs me every time he sees me?"

"How does Chris's K-9 deal with your cats?"

Fiona's cheeks flushed. "We're working that out."

"Good. He's a good guy. Bye and thanks, Fiona." Nicholas strolled down the hallway. When his cell rang, he expected it to be Dan, who'd been going over security video at the White House, with news about Miss Chick's assailant, but he noticed it was Selena. He quickly answered, "How's the cleaning going?"

"Tedious. I know what the intruder took yesterday at my house."

FOUR

Thirty minutes after calling Nicholas, Selena opened her front door to him and Max. "Come in. Did you break any speed limits getting here?"

"I'm a law-enforcement officer. I know better unless in pursuit of a criminal." He flashed his dynamite smile.

And for a few seconds all the tension and weariness fled Selena as they stared at each other. When Max barked, as though he knew they needed to focus on what had brought Nicholas to her house in the first place, Selena broke eye contact and turned her attention to the dog. "It's good to see you, Max." She petted him and rubbed him behind the ears.

"He isn't going to want to leave if you continue that too long," Nicholas said with a laugh.

She peered up at Nicholas, grinning. "I doubt anyone could sway him from his duties with all his training. I've seen him at work at the White House." She straightened, determined to get down to business. She didn't like the feelings of attraction Nicholas could generate in her. She had to remember he suspected her of helping Erin, and he had a job to do.

She stepped to the side and allowed him to enter, then shut the door. When she swung around, her messy living room, such an alien sight for her, chased away the lightness she'd felt at seeing Nicholas. He was here on business. "I've been working on righting the rooms upstairs. I haven't made my way down here yet."

"Are you sure that your personal computer tablet is missing?"

"I keep it in my bedroom in the drawer of my nightstand on the right. You can't tell from all this chaos, but I'm highly organized and everything has a place."

"The intruder took your tablet but not your laptop. Why? What was on the tablet that wasn't on your laptop?"

She picked her way through the shattered items on the floor, found the couch cushions and put them back where they belonged, then sat. She'd only been cleaning and straightening for a few hours, but after yesterday, she was tired. Usually she could keep going and push through the exhaustion, but not today.

Before Nicholas settled at the opposite end of the sofa, he fixed the two chairs. "For someone who is highly organized, this must be a disturbing sight."

"Yes. Even as a child I kept everything straight. It gave me a sense of control." The second she said that last sentence she gritted her teeth, afraid of what else she would spill about herself. She must be wearier than she realized. She had to remember Nicholas wanted to capture Erin; Selena wanted to free her.

"I wish it were that simple. The older I get, the more I realize we control little in our lives."

"Yeah, I know. Only our attitude and how we respond to what happens around us. But I wish I could control more. Then I would wish this all away, and I wouldn't have to spend my days off cleaning up this mess." As words poured from her, she sat back, amazed she was saying this to Nicholas. What was it about him that made her feel she could trust him? His own words had given her reason not to. She'd remembered what he'd said in the underground parking garage yesterday.

My team has looked into all the possibilities while searching for Erin, so being a friend and a family member, you would obviously be on that list. And if I was perfectly honest, at first that is why I initiated several conversations with you lately.

"I can stay and help. I want to make sure the tablet is the only thing missing."

She bit down on her bottom lip. The temptation to accept his offer was strong.

"Everyone needs help from time to time. Let me help you, Selena."

His calm countenance soothed her, and before she realized what she was doing, she nodded.

"Before we get to work, tell me what was on the tablet."

He wouldn't be happy about what she was about to say, but if that was the reason behind the break-in, she wanted him to know. She drew in a deep, composing breath. "I've been looking into the cases Michael was working on right before he was killed. I think there could be a tie to one of them and his murder."

"Which ones?" His mouth pulled into a thin, firm line.

"There were three that look promising, but one of them was a dead end."

"The Capitol K-9 Unit has been delving into all of Michael's activities, and so far we have come up with nothing, so why do you think two cases are still viable leads?"

"One of them is the Huntington case."

"The man convicted of selling intelligence secrets is guilty. All the evidence pointed to him."

Selena nodded. "But Sid Huntington insists he's innocent, that someone set him up to be the fall guy, and Michael believed him."

Nicholas shook his head. "Michael was

wrong. I'm familiar with that case. I went through it when we looked at what Michael was working on at the time of his murder."

"Michael's secretary told me that he was on the trail of a new piece of evidence. He'd been excited about the possible lead."

"But she didn't know what it was?"

"No, and I haven't been able to find out what it was."

"So other than that, Huntington looks guilty to you?"

"Yes." She squeezed her hands into fists. Listening to herself made even her think she was grasping for an answer.

Frown lines grooved his forehead. "What's the other case?"

Selena hesitated. This one involved her uncle, and she'd been putting it off, delving into all the others first because she didn't want to make their precarious relationship any worse. Only in the past couple of weeks had she turned to the Littleton case. "It's another one that Michael was working on overturning the conviction."

"The Littleton case?"

Selena nodded.

"I'm not that familiar with it. Another K-9 officer looked into that one."

"Greg Littleton was sent to prison for murdering Saul Rather. Saul was a young intern for my uncle. He'd been with him only two months."

"What was Littleton's connection to Rather?"

"He was the custodian at Saul's apartment complex." Selena rose. "I fixed some coffee after talking to you on the phone. Do you want some?"

"Yes, please."

She escaped into the kitchen, needing time to decide what to tell him. There was no way her uncle was involved. The intern on her uncle's staff hadn't been there that long. He ranked at the bottom of the office personnel, doing all the work no one else wanted to do. She doubted her uncle had had any dealings with the young man.

"What was Michael Jeffries doing for Littleton?"

The question took Selena by surprise. She spun around, her hand over her heart. "I didn't hear you come in here."

"Sorry. I learned to be silent when I was a Navy SEAL."

She leaned against the counter, the thump of her heartbeat calming. "Littleton had an appeal, and Michael took over the case from Greg's court-appointed attorney. His secretary told me Michael felt the guy botched the case from the beginning."

"Is that why Michael thought Littleton was innocent?"

"The evidence was circumstantial. Greg found Saul Rather's body in the parking lot early in the morning. Minutes before, Greg heard what he thought was a car backfiring. When a tenant found them, Greg was kneeling next to Saul's body. Greg's prints were the only ones on the gun. Greg testified he moved it when he checked to see if Saul was alive."

"That's what he was convicted on?"

"Greg isn't the smartest person. He was shocked at finding a body and wasn't thinking straight."

"So what was his motive?"

"The night before, Saul and Greg had a fight near the apartment's pool. Some of the tenants witnessed it. Saul accused Greg of coming into his apartment and stealing from him. He was going to talk to the management office about firing Greg."

Nicholas scowled. "No one else had a motive?"

"Not that the police could find, but I'm not so sure they looked too hard. With the murder of a senator's staff member, they wanted to close it quickly. I believe my uncle put some pressure on them, too. I don't think he wanted his name in the paper associated with a murder victim. He was up for reelection at that time. This all happened almost two years ago. Greg's been in jail since the crime."

"Greg? You keep saying his first name as if you know him. Do you?"

She turned toward the counter and reached

for a mug for Nicholas, filling it and topping off hers.

"Selena, are you avoiding my question?"

Her grip on the coffeepot handle tightened. She put the glass carafe down and passed him his mug. "I have met him."

"When? How?"

"At the end of last week, I went to see him at the prison, and we talked for a while. I used the fact I was the niece of a US senator to have a quiet, extended time to interview Greg and determine if I agree with Michael."

One of his eyebrows shot up. "And?"

"I think he's innocent."

Nicholas took a sip of his coffee. "Why?"

"For one thing, the thief in the apartment complex was discovered not long after Greg was convicted. Michael followed up on that and discovered the items stolen from Saul's apartment were pawned by the man caught, so Littleton was innocent of stealing from Saul. No motive. But the assistant DA said that didn't really prove anything. The threat of being fired was enough of a motive. People have killed for less."

"True."

"There's only so much I can glean from the court records and Michael's secretary's memory. My thoughts and notes of the meeting were on the stolen computer tablet. I'm going back out to talk to Littleton. I know of a couple of witnesses who testified to the argument between the victim and Greg, but there were others who weren't at the trial. I'm thinking about talking to some of those people as well as the others and—"

"Hold it right there." He put up his finger close to her mouth but not touching it. "You are *not* to investigate anything involved in Michael's case, especially now. Have you forgotten someone broke into your house?"

She squared her shoulders and narrowed her eyes at him. "I don't know if your team has really investigated Michael and the possible motives for his murder. If Erin isn't the killer, I think you all believe someone was after the congressman and Michael got in the way."

Nicholas met her intense gaze with his own. "It's more likely that the congressman has made enemies more than his son. Remember he was a victim, too."

"From what I know of the crime, the congressman came outside after his son was killed and he was shot then. That sounds like someone was after Michael, not Congressman Jeffries."

"True. We have to look at all the possibilities." Nicholas glanced away for a few seconds. "What did Greg tell you exactly?"

She frowned. "A lot of what I told you. He gave me some names, but I can't remember all of them. As I said earlier, I'd written them down along with other notes then transferred them to my tablet. That's one of the reasons I need to go back. That, and Greg was going to try to remember any encounters with the delivery boy who was the real thief at the apartment complex."

"Is Littleton the one who told you about the pawnshop where the perpetrator was fencing the stolen goods?"

"No, I told him. He didn't know anything about it. Michael's secretary told me. It was something Michael discovered a few days before his death. Ask the officer who looked into the case if he even knew about the pawnshop. He might not have had all the information on the case at the time of Michael's murder."

Nicholas stepped closer to her, invading her personal space. "I will. Does that satisfy you?"

She wouldn't move back as was her normal tendency when someone came too near. Holding her ground, she lifted her mug and took a long drink of her now-lukewarm coffee. "Until all my questions are answered, no. I'm concerned for Erin, so I will do what I must to prove her innocence."

He thrust his face closer. "Do you want to end up dead like Michael?"

Selena sucked in a ragged breath and backed away. "I told Greg I would come see him again and I intend to. I also asked him to go over the time from right before the fight to when the police showed up. Including if he could remember seeing anyone who wasn't a tenant at the apartment complex."

"I'm sure the cops already did that."

"But now he has all the time in the world to go over it. When a person is afraid, he can suppress some thoughts."

Nicholas placed his mug on the counter, putting more space between them while he kneaded his nape. "What if I help you? Will you not do anything without me?"

"Are you going to be open-minded or are you going to try at every turn to persuade me to drop my investigation?"

He paused for a long moment, his dark eyes fixed on her. "I'll be there to protect you and bounce ideas off of. Is that okay?"

"Yeah. Because I'm going to the prison on Thursday and you're welcome to come with me." She wouldn't admit to him that she was concerned after someone had been in her office and her house, picking through her possessions. She kept her journal on her tablet, writing her personal thoughts as well as the developments and questions about Michael's murder and possible suspects. She felt violated all over again, thinking about a person reading through her private thoughts. She shuddered.

"Are you okay? Maybe you should rest. You do have a mild concussion."

She smiled, trying not to think of her journal

in someone else's hands. "Is that why my head is pounding? I'd hoped if I ignored it, the headache would go away." She glanced at the kitchen clock. "Time for another pain reliever, and then I need to get back to work straightening up this place."

"I have a suggestion. Why don't you lie down and rest while I at least put your furniture back and straighten some. It might make it easier for you to go through your belongings later."

"Don't you have to work?"

"It's nearly noon, so I'm on my lunch break."

She studied him, his commanding presence appealing at a time when she felt vulnerable. "Fine, if you make sure I only nap for half an hour. I finished upstairs, but look at all this. I've got too much to do, so I can't rest long, and someone is coming at one to install the alarm system."

"That's good he's coming so quickly."

As she made her way to her bedroom, she glanced over her shoulder at Max, at attention, by the front door, then mounted the stairs. She sensed Nicholas watching her from the bottom of the steps, but she wouldn't look back to check. In the bathroom, she swallowed an over-the-counter pain reliever and some water then stretched out on her bed, hoping the tap dancing inside her head would subside. The only reason she'd agreed to his assistance was because she needed her house put back right as fast as possible. The sight of the chaos made her feel exposed and weak. She'd fought hard these past years not to be either.

"Well, Max, it's just you and me to clean this up as much as possible while she's sleeping. She'll probably kick us out once she gets up." Nicholas started at one end of the large living area, returning books strewn near the bookcase. He might not put them back in the right order, but they would at least be off the floor.

As he began picking up items and the small pieces of furniture that were still turned over, he checked for any sign of the tablet. The fact that it was the only thing missing—at least so far—meant this break-in could be tied to the Jeffries murder somehow. Or tied to Michael Jeffries, anyway. Although he didn't believe as Selena did in the connection, he'd been taught to investigate every lead. What if it led to the break the team needed?

Although the Capitol K-9 Unit was working other cases, this one was important to their captain, and therefore the team. Congressman Jeffries had helped Captain Gavin McCord as a child. He owed the man a lot. Nicholas wasn't as fond of Congressman Jeffries, who he suspected might have taken bribes in the past, and Gavin had asked him to withhold judgment until there was evidence that Jeffries was involved in anything shady.

Right now, he had to figure out the connection between Selena's missing tablet and Michael Jeffries's murder. *Was* there something to the Littleton case as Selena hoped? There was the connection to Senator Eagleton, which might be something—or nothing. Selena wanted to prove her cousin was innocent, so she was looking for anything to throw suspicion somewhere else. He wasn't sure what to think, but he did know that someone out there didn't like what Selena was doing. She might not appreciate it, but he was going to hang around as much as he could because he couldn't shake the feeling she could be in danger. What if the person who took the tablet didn't like what he or she found and decided to stop Selena's snooping permanently? What if Littleton was innocent and the murderer knew what Selena was doing? That was exactly what Selena thought might have gotten Michael Jeffries killed.

When Nicholas finished the living room and started on the kitchen, the doorbell rang. He looked at the wall clock and realized it was ten to one. He hurried to the front door, checked who it was through the peephole and let the guy from the alarm company into the house.

"Miss Barrow is upstairs. I'll get her for

you." Nicholas turned to Max next to him and added, "Guard."

The man's eyes widened.

"A precaution after what has happened here. Stay right there, and you'll be fine."

Nicholas took the stairs two at a time and knocked on Selena's bedroom door. When she didn't answer, he rapped louder the second time.

She flung the door open, a drowsy look on her face. "You let me oversleep."

"Sorry. I was working and lost track of time. The alarm guy is here."

She rushed into the hallway, finger combing her long, brown hair.

As she descended the staircase, he asked, "How's your headache?"

"Better."

He caught up with her at the bottom of the steps. "Good. I can finish in the kitchen while you talk with the man."

She peered across the room and slanted a glance at Nicholas. "You have Max guarding him?"

He shrugged. "You can't be too careful."

"Yes, you can." She headed toward the man. "Mr. Woods, thank you so much for fitting me in." She held out her hand, and they shook. "My friend is being overly protective. Call Max off, Nicholas."

"Come." After Max trotted to Nicholas's side, he gave him a treat. "Good boy."

While Selena talked with Mr. Woods, Nicholas went into the kitchen and worked, but he kept Max at the door lying down facing her and the alarm guy.

When she came into the room minus Mr. Woods, Nicholas asked, "Is he gone?"

"Why don't you ask Max? He was watching us the whole time."

"I suspect everyone."

"I know you do, me included."

"Not in this."

"Oh, that's nice," she said in a sarcastic tone. "What do you know about this Mr. Woods? Did you just call anyone in the Yellow Pages?"

"He was recommended by the chief of staff and no doubt the reason he has agreed to come back in an hour with his equipment and install the system today. No thanks to you and Max." She placed her fists on her waist, her lips drawn in a narrow line.

"Okay, I might have been a little overzealous, but I'd rather be that than let anything happen to you."

Her fierce expression and stance relaxed. "I don't have the energy to be mad at you right now."

"Good." He grinned, liking her spunk. "Tell

you what. I'll go get us something to eat. I saw a hamburger place not too far from here."

"They have delicious burgers, and I'll take some fries, too."

He started for the front door. "Lock the door behind me. And I'm leaving Max to keep you company."

"We'll try not to have too much fun while you're gone."

Nicholas chuckled as he left the house, waiting to hear the sound of the lock clicking into place. At his SUV he paused and scanned the area. No cars parked along the street and only a couple in driveways. Nothing set off alarm bells.

On Thursday afternoon, Nicholas sat next to Selena in an interview room at the prison while they waited for Greg Littleton to be escorted to them.

"I thought after we see Greg we could grab dinner before I take you home," Nicholas said.

"You haven't been far from my side much except when you had to go in to work. Surprisingly not a lot. You'd think you had these past few days off." She shot him a look. "You haven't been outside my house sleeping like that first night, have you?"

"No, you have a good alarm system and Max for a roommate when I leave."

Which had only been about eight hours the

last two nights. "Okay, spill it. I can take care of myself. I have a gun and that good alarm system you mentioned."

"I told my captain about what's going on, and he agrees I need to keep a close eye on you. I can review security tapes from my laptop."

"What have you found about the fake Miss Chick?"

"Not much other than what we already know. The person knew how to avoid the cameras, which indicates a certain knowledge of the West Wing. A slender, unidentified woman, five-nine or ten with long wavy black hair is the person I suspect assaulted Tara Wilkins in the restroom. We're going through the video at the entrances, but we haven't found her."

"A disguise?"

"Probably."

"How about General Meyer's office?" Selena asked, wondering if the same person had broken in there.

"I can't say, but progress is being made. We're narrowing the long list down. But no one fits the description of the suspect in Tara Wilkins's case."

She twisted toward him as the door opened. "You don't have to keep babysitting me. I'm going to work tomorrow now that my house is back to normal," she whispered, then glanced toward Greg shuffling into the room.

After the guard left and took up a post outside the door, Selena gestured toward Nicholas. "This is Nicholas Cole. He works for the Capitol K-9 Unit and has an interest in your case."

Greg looked from Selena to Nicholas. "You mean, someone else believes I'm innocent?"

"I won't go as far as that, but I think there may be more to your situation. Why don't you tell me what happened from the time you and Saul Rather got into an argument by the pool."

While Greg told Nicholas what he had said to her last week, Selena took notes, listening closely to determine if he added anything new. She noticed the weary set to the thin, forty-two-year-old man's shoulders and the tired lines in his face. His skin had a pasty pallor to it, and his brown hair had grayed at the temples. Different from the photo of the man at his trial she'd studied before she'd come to see him a week ago.

As Greg finished, disappointment weaved through her. He'd said nothing new. Nothing new that she could recall, and that was the problem. She couldn't check her notes on her tablet. "Can you tell me the names of the people you remember were with you at the pool that evening when Saul confronted you?"

She jotted down their names, recalling no changes from the last time she'd asked.

"I also remember that Tabitha Miller and a couple of her female friends came out onto her balcony while Saul Rather was yelling at me," Greg said. "I didn't think to mention that before since Tabitha and her friends weren't right there at the pool like the others and only on the balcony for a minute. I tried to visualize like you said to, but that's all I came up with."

She straightened at the same time Nicholas did. Tabitha Miller was an aide for Congressman Jeffries. "She lives there at the apartment complex?"

"Yes, at least two years ago."

Selena jotted down the information, making a note to check and see if she still lived there.

"Did you recognize any of the other women with her? Did they live at the apartment complex?" Nicholas gave her a look that told her to let him do the interviewing.

Selena bit the inside of her cheek to keep from saying anything.

"No to both questions. One of the ladies I'd never seen, but I remember the other had come once before."

"I'm surprised you have such a good memory of who was there." Nicholas lounged back in his chair, taking in Greg's every nuance.

"When a person gets chewed out in front of people, they tend to look around, embarrassed, to see who heard. At least that's my experience. Do you think I'd kill the guy with so many witnesses watching the argument and able to testify to a motive for me to kill him?"

"It's happened before." Nicholas crossed his arms. "Can you think of anything else about that twenty-four hours? Why did you go to the parking garage so early the next morning?"

"I told the police when they picked me up I received a call about a car with a smashed window."

Selena stared at Nicholas. "I didn't know that. I didn't find it in the record. Greg, did your lawyer bring that detail up at the trial? I don't remember it in the court records."

"No one seemed to think that information meant anything. Just something to cover my tracks. There wasn't a car with a smashed window."

"Do you remember if it was a female or male voice who called you?" Nicholas asked, interest on his face.

Greg thought for a long moment, his lips pursed. "I'm not sure. It was a gruff voice. I think."

Nicholas took out his business card. "If you come up with anything new, give me a call."

"So that's important to my case?"

"It could be. Remember everything and tell us, even if you don't think it's important. It might all fit together. One piece of the puzzle."

For a few seconds Greg's usual defeated

expression vanished. "I will. Thank you. Both of you."

Ten minutes later, Nicholas opened his SUV door for Selena. When he came around and slid behind the steering wheel, she asked, "What do you think? We need to go talk to Tabitha Miller as soon as possible. She works for Congressman Jeffries. What if Michael found that out and came over to talk to his dad about her? You see the connection?"

He started the car then angled toward her. "Just because one of the witnesses to the fight worked for Congressman Jeffries doesn't mean there's a connection to Michael's murder. Don't get your hopes up. And you are *not* going to talk to her. I am. Understood?"

"Only if you'll tell me what she says. She fits. She has access to the West Wing and would know its layout. She is about the height of Miss Chick."

"Slow down. When we get back to your house, we'll discuss the next steps." He sliced her a stern look. "The only reason I'm even including you in that discussion is that I'm afraid you'll go off half-cocked, pursuing your own investigation. Even if Michael talked with Tabitha, that doesn't mean anything except he was following every lead and talking to every witness to the fight."

"I hate to see Greg Littleton in prison for a

crime he didn't commit. Just as I hate to see my cousin out there being hunted for one she didn't do."

"It must be nice that you know all that for sure. I need evidence to prove it. Not theories and a woman's intuition."

"My, you are cynical."

He stopped at a red light and swung his full attention to her. "And you aren't? I've read your dossier. I know what kind of childhood you had. A tough one."

Surprised, she felt the color drain from her face while her heartbeat slowed for a few seconds before revving up as anger swelled in her. "Tough? I guess compared to yours it was. I wasn't born with a silver spoon in my mouth."

His hands gripped the steering wheel so tight his knuckles whitened. "So I guess we both know the facts of each other's background. For the record, the only reason I looked into your past was because of the case."

"The same reason for me. You were involved in the Jeffries case. I do have a few connections, working in the White House."

He clamped his teeth down so hard that a muscle in his cheek twitched. He made a left turn and kept his focus on the road. Silence ruled for the next five minutes, with Nicholas glancing at the rearview mirror every thirty seconds.

Selena tensed, feeling his alertness spike. "What's going on?"

He swerved across a lane of traffic and took a hard right, the tires screeching. "We're being followed."

FIVE

"Who's following us? Where?" Selena twisted around, looking out the rear window.

Nicholas increased his speed and made another turn. "The white car's coming around the corner. Hold on. We're going for a little ride."

He'd seen that same car when they'd left the prison. Then it disappeared but reappeared a few streets before he stopped at the light.

"Do you think someone followed us to the prison?" Selena kept peering back as Nicholas pushed the speed limit when he finally left a residential area.

"I don't think so. We picked this tail up at the prison." Which made him wonder how. Why? Maybe Selena was on to something about Littleton. This all started after she first visited the man who was convicted of killing one of Senator Eagleton's interns. Everything led back to Eagleton and Jeffries.

He made a quick decision and swerved left

onto a side street, then right and accelerated down an alley. Another right followed by a sharp turn, which brought him back to the original street.

"I don't see the car behind us. I think you lost him." Selena straightened in her seat.

"Not for long." Nicholas went down the side street a second time. "We're going hunting. I want to know who is so interested in us."

"Good. We need answers."

He chuckled. "We?"

"Yes, you said we would work together on Littleton's case, or do you want me to do it alone? I will if I have to."

He continued down the side street, searching for the white car. "You drive a hard bargain, which doesn't surprise me. All I can promise is that I'll keep you informed of what I discover concerning Littleton."

"And Erin?"

"I can't, for obvious reasons."

"Because you still think I'm helping her. Is that the real reason you're taking such an active role in *protecting* me?"

Was it? Good question. If he were honest, no. There was something about Selena that attracted him. "It's more complicated than that."

"That's a cop-out."

He spied the rear of a white car turning up ahead and passed the vehicle in front of him.

Selena leaned forward. "Is that our guy?"

"I think so." Nicholas took the corner then pressed down on the accelerator, gaining on the car. "Jot down the license-plate numbers." Suddenly the Dodge shot forward. "I think he knows we're here. Hang on."

Selena dug into her purse and withdrew the pad she'd used at the prison. "I got the numbers."

For the next ten minutes, the Dodge weaved through traffic, ran a stop sign and took Nicholas on a merry chase. He closed the distance between the two vehicles when the white car flew through a light when it turned red. Nicholas slammed on his brakes as a school bus pulled into the intersection.

Selena jerked forward, her seat belt halting her.

Heartbeat racing, fed by the flow of adrenaline into his system, Nicholas eased his tight grip on the steering wheel and uncurled his fingers. "Are you okay?"

"Fine."

"We've probably lost him."

The light flashed green. Nicholas looked both ways then crossed the intersection, heading in the direction the Dodge had gone.

After a twenty-minute search of the surrounding streets, he pulled over to the curb and called Fiona at headquarters. "I need a favor."

"Anything for you, if you promise to bring Max by to see me next time y'all are here."

"I thought you were a cat person."

"I have cats, but I'm an animal lover."

"Same here."

"What do you need? Then I'll give you an update on those videos I've been going through."

Fiona was also going through the same ones he was. Two sets of eyes were better than one. "I have a Virginia license plate I need you to run down for me." Nicholas took the sheet Selena handed him and recited the three letters then four numbers.

"Wait. It shouldn't take long. My fingers are dancing across the keys as we speak." A minute later she said, "I've got it. The owner is Benny Goodwin." Then she gave him the address associated with the license plate.

"Thanks. Will you do another favor for me?"

"I'm already on it. I'll pull up what I can on Mr. Goodwin and call you back."

Nicholas disconnected with Fiona. "I'll have something soon on the guy who owns the Dodge. Do you know a Benny Goodwin?"

Selena shook her head.

"Let's grab something to eat. I want to know about this guy before I pay him a visit."

"Don't you mean we?"

He didn't want to argue with her right now, but he wouldn't put her in danger no matter what she wanted. "Let's check out that café at the end of the block. I forgot to grab lunch before coming to pick you up."

"I'm not going to let you change the subject," she said as Nicholas exited his SUV, scoping out the streets with quaint shops.

If he ignored the question, maybe she would get tired of asking. He rounded the hood and waited for her to climb out of the Tahoe. "I'm thinking a nice big piece of pie. I love pie. Not many I won't eat."

She gave him a frown and marched toward the restaurant ahead of him. Her body language shouted frustration and anger. He didn't care. He wouldn't put her in danger. He would let her help when he thought the situation wasn't risky.

As she entered the café, his cell rang. He noted it was Fiona. "Tell me you have the low-down on Benny Goodwin."

"When haven't I given you the info you needed? He's a private investigator with an office in Arlington. Do you want the address?"

"You're the best tech support a team could have."

Fiona laughed and gave him the information. "He has a thriving business, from what I can gather, mostly divorce cases."

"Thanks. I won't forget to bring you a chai tea latte and Max next time I come to headquarters."

Nicholas pocketed his cell and headed into

the restaurant, a fifties throwback with a jukebox, red booths and pictures of films from that era. Selena sat in a booth with a *Rebel Without a Cause* poster on the wall nearby. He was beginning to think of her as a rebel *with* a cause.

He slid in across from her, opened the menu and spied the waitress coming toward them. "Let's talk after we order."

"What would you two like?" The older woman retrieved a pencil from over her left ear.

"What's your specialty?" Nicholas asked, feeling Selena's glare on him.

"Chicken-fried steak and mashed potatoes with gravy. Also the hamburgers."

"How about pies? We don't have time for dinner." Selena set the menu on the table. "Which is the best?"

"Blackberry is my favorite, but most of our customers order the cherry pie."

"How's the chocolate one?" Selena folded her arms over her chest.

"Good. You can't go wrong with any of them."

"I'll take the cherry pie with vanilla ice cream." Nicholas placed his menu on top of Selena's. "And a cup of black coffee. It smells delicious." That scent fused with baking bread and grilling meat. His stomach rumbled.

"How about you, miss?"

"The chocolate pie would be great with a cup of coffee."

When the waitress left, Selena leaned forward. "I want to go with you to see Benny Goodwin. The name doesn't sound familiar, but I might know him or have seen him around."

"Here. I've got his driver's-license photo." He withdrew his cell and clicked on the one Fiona had sent. "Not a good picture. Looks like a mug shot."

Selena took the phone and studied the screen. "No. He's not familiar. I still want to go with you."

"You're as persistent as the salmon returning home."

She pressed her lips together and glared at him.

"I found out from Fiona that he's a private eye, so I don't see why you can't come with me."

Her eyes brightened. "Really?"

"Yes. After I have my pie. Cherry is my favorite."

"I like cherry, too, but chocolate fits my mood."

"It does?"

"I like to eat chocolate when I'm stressed or frustrated. I'm both at the moment."

"I'm taking you to see Benny Goodwin."

"I think this little bump in our working relationship is an indication of more to come."

He leaned forward, lacing his fingers together,

his arms on the table. "You are *not* a law-en-forcement officer. I won't put you in danger."

She bent closer to him, their heads inches away. "You are *not* my keeper. I've tolerated your presence in this, but you can't stop me from pursuing my own inquiries. I was doing just fine by myself."

Nicholas ground his teeth together and lounged back. He wasn't going to be drawn into a battle with Selena. "Ah, I see our pie is coming."

She huffed and sat stiffly against the cushion. "I'm thinking of having two pieces."

She was one stubborn lady, but she'd met her match with him.

"Now I see why you let me come. His office is in a nice area. He obviously must be success-ful at his job." Selena let Nicholas open the main door to a three-story renovated redbrick house that had been turned into a commercial build-ing. She noticed several lawyers on the plaque of tenants. Smart move on Mr. Goodwin's part. Attorneys often used private investigators.

Nicholas followed her inside but didn't re-spond to her statement. In fact, through the stop at the diner and the drive to this place, he'd been silent. He wasn't happy with her. Every part of him screamed that. She didn't care. She was the one who had grown up in a tough, gang-infested area, while he'd lived on an estate in Maryland with all his needs met. He hadn't gone hungry or feared every time he'd left his home that he could be shot. She'd done her research on him in the past couple of days. His grandfather had been a senator and had come from a long line of members of Congress. He'd been influential and wealthy—like her mother's family. So why in the world was he working as a cop, albeit in an elite unit handpicked by a former general?

That question taunted her as they made their way to the second floor where Mr. Goodwin had his office. After the interview, she would ask Nicholas. Otherwise it would bug her until she found out. A nasty habit that had gotten her into trouble occasionally.

She approached the private eye's secretary a few steps ahead of Nicholas and said before he could, "We are here to see Mr. Goodwin." Nicholas wouldn't have known about Littleton and the possible importance of him to the Jeffries case without her. The motive for Michael Jeffries's murder might very well be due to Michael's work to set Littleton free from prison and find the real killer of Senator Eagleton's aide. She needed Nicholas to realize she was part of the investigation.

"Do you have an appointment?" the young woman, probably no more than twenty, asked while smacking her gum. "He's on the phone right now."

Nicholas stepped next to Selena. "No, but you might tell him we're the two he was following earlier today and would like a word with him. Now."

The secretary's eyes grew round, sliding a glance toward her employer's door.

Nicholas showed her his badge. "This is police business."

The young woman jumped to her feet and hurried into Mr. Goodwin's office. When she came back in half a minute, she said, "He can see you now."

"Does that badge always do the trick?" Selena whispered as she made her way to the door.

"Not always. Sometimes it sends a person in flight." Nicholas entered a room with folders and photos stacked on a messy desk.

The older man behind it was hurriedly clearing it off. When he looked up, he said, "I told Betsy to give me five minutes. I was working on a case." He gestured to the papers and pictures spread out before him.

"Does the case have anything to do with following Miss Barrow and me?" Nicholas flipped open his badge and showed it to Mr. Goodwin.

The man's face paled, and he sank into his chair. "There's nothing illegal about driving on the streets. You can't prove I was following you two."

Nicholas took a seat in one of the chairs in front of the desk. "There is when you run a stop sign and a red light. You drove recklessly and almost hit a school bus full of children. That wouldn't look too good on the news."

"You aren't an Arlington police officer. You have no jurisdiction here."

"But I know the chief of police as well as a number of officers in Arlington, not to mention I work at the White House."

Selena hadn't thought the man's face could get any paler, but Mr. Goodwin's did.

"What do you want?" The private detective's voice quavered.

"Why were you following us today?" Selena blurted out before Nicholas could say anything.

Mr. Goodwin remained silent for a long moment then finally said, "I can't break confidentiality."

Nicholas sat forward. "There will be enough evidence to make an arrest once the police review the traffic cam. When I'm finished with you, you might lose your driver's license. How are you going to do your work without one?"

Selena wondered if Nicholas could do that. If she were Mr. Goodwin, she'd believe him because of the hard edge to Nicholas's words and the fierce look on his face.

"This involves the attempted murder of a high-ranking government official."

Selena marveled at how the impression of "don't mess with me" came across loud and clear from Nicholas. Mr. Goodwin shook.

"I don't want any trouble. I was called because you two went to visit Greg Littleton. I'm notified when someone comes to see him, and I follow them to see who they are and where they go."

"Who hired you?"

"I can't tell you."

Nicholas took out his cell phone, rose and leaned over Mr. Goodwin's desk. "I'll give you ten seconds to tell me who hired you. If you don't, I'm calling the police chief."

The private detective blinked rapidly. "I can't…"

Nicholas punched in two numbers.

"I can't get another ticket. Please."

Nicholas pushed two more buttons.

"Senator Eagleton's office," Mr. Goodwin shouted.

Why would her uncle want to know?

"Who hired you? Who set this up?" Selena clenched the arms of the chair.

"I don't know. My secretary took the call and set it up a couple of months ago. Other than Littleton's mother, you are the only one who has visited him. Until today, when he came with you." Mr. Goodwin tossed his head toward Nicholas.

"How do you report to the person who hired you?" she fired another question at the private investigator.

"I call a number and leave a message."

"Don't you think that's strange you don't talk to someone personally?"

Mr. Goodwin lifted his shoulders in a shrug. "Miss, in this job, I've dealt with some strange people."

"How are you paid?" Nicholas sat again in the chair next to Selena.

"Cash, almost immediately after each time I've reported in. The amount varies on how much time I spend finding out who the person is and basic information on them. I won't call the number about today." Mr. Goodwin stared at Nicholas. "Your name won't be mentioned."

"But you have mentioned my associate?"

"Yes. Not long ago." The man turned to her. "Selena Barrow, White House tour director."

Nicholas stood. "Please write down the number you called and then make a call to it and report that we visited Littleton today."

After Mr. Goodwin jotted something on the piece of paper and gave it to Nicholas, the detective picked up his phone and made the call. He was on the line two minutes, giving the details of who went to see Littleton, then he hung up.

"I tried to trace the number once. Prepaid cell phone. I couldn't."

"We're leaving right after we talk with your secretary." Nicholas waited while Selena rose and started for the door. "Keep doing what you're doing. Call me when you receive payment for the tip. I'll need to check the envelope. Don't let anyone know about this chat, not even your secretary."

"I won't. I don't want to lose any business over it. Times are tough and rent is high here."

Out in the reception area, Nicholas smiled at the young secretary and half leaned, half sat on the side of her desk. "Do you remember anything about who set up the account with Senator Eagleton's office a couple of months ago?"

As she continued to chew and snap her gum, the woman scrunched her forehead and tapped her chin with a fingernail with hot-pink polish on it. She finally shook her head.

"A man or woman? This is important," Nicholas said with a slight Southern drawl.

"I think a man... No, wait, a female. I don't believe I got a name."

Nicholas took out a business card and wrote his cell number on the back. "Call me—if you remember anything." He winked and straightened. "Good day, Betsy."

The young woman's cheeks reddened. "I will—" she looked at the card "—Nicholas."

Out in the hallway, Selena rolled her eyes and laughed. "You're a smooth operator, Nicolas Cole."

"It's a tough job, but someone has to do it." He gave her a wink and headed for the stairs.

Back in his SUV, Selena relaxed for the first time since the private detective had started following them. "I have some steaks at home. Why don't we skip going out to dinner? I'm not hungry right now since I ate the pie. I'm sure Max is wondering where we went without him."

"He's probably thrilled. He got an afternoon off."

"Well, not exactly. He's guarding my house."

"True. He's learned to protect his territory. Honestly, I don't think anyone will come back. They searched thoroughly the first time."

"Yeah, I think they got what they were looking for." Selena took in his strong profile and liked what she saw. Not movie-star handsome but definitely heart-stopping when he smiled and his dark chocolate–colored eyes sparkled.

When Nicholas turned onto her street, she broke the silence of the past ten minutes. "So what are we going to do next? Go see my uncle?"

"No." He pulled into her driveway. "I'll look into this lead."

"Have you met my uncle?"

"Once."

"He's a very private man. We may not have

a great relationship, but I am his niece." She didn't want Nicholas interviewing him. She couldn't believe her uncle would order her house searched. His method would have been to come see her and demand to know why she was investigating Littleton's case. He'd want to view what evidence she'd collected because Erin was his daughter, and he'd always loved her. He would see she was trying to prove Erin was innocent and might even want to take over Littleton's case. This might be the time she could mend the breach between—

"What's wrong?"

"Nothing. Just thinking about my uncle."

"I don't want anyone to think you're investigating Littleton on your own."

"Okay. Then we go together. I'm conceding Tabitha to you but not my uncle." She'd seen how Nicholas got women to talk. Perhaps he'd be able to charm information out of Congressman Jeffries's aide and find out what she remembered about the argument between Littleton and the murdered intern.

He stared at her as though probing her reasons behind the request. "Why is this important to you?"

For a moment she didn't know if she could tell him, but it was imperative since she had gotten close to Erin. She'd wanted to be part of a family. She was determined to help Erin come back safely, with her name cleared. If her uncle didn't want to have anything to do with her, so be it. She would be satisfied with being close with Erin.

"Selena?"

She angled toward him. "I have a letter from my mother written when she was dying from alcohol poisoning, begging me to give it to her brother and make sure he read it. I'm afraid with the way our relationship is now, he would take it and tear it up without reading. I want to fulfill this last obligation to my mother then I'll be…" She swallowed back the word *free* and averted her gaze.

"You'll be what?" he said in a gentle voice.

"Free of my past. I washed my hands of dealing with my mom's drinking. I refused to see her until the hospital called and told me she was dying. I should have been there for her." What was it about Nicholas that she said out loud something she had been suppressing and struggling with since her mother had died three years ago?

He touched her arm and drew her around so their gazes linked. "I'm sorry. Our past can play with our minds sometimes."

"My childhood wasn't anything like yours."

"Do you think I had an easy time while growing up?"

"Did you go without food for a couple of days at a time?"

He pulled back from her, all feelings wiped from his expression. "I won't play one-up with you. No, my life was different from yours, but it had its challenges."

His blank look, which had chased away the earlier concern, bothered her. "I'm sorry. I know that just because you came from a wealthy family doesn't guarantee an easy life. I haven't walked in your shoes. I shouldn't have judged."

His hands on the steering wheel, his body facing forward, he fixed his gaze on something beyond the windshield. "Let's start over. Is the steak dinner still on the table?"

"Yes, I'll use the microwave to defrost them. I can put a couple of baking potatoes in the oven and make salad."

He sent her that special smile, dimples appearing in his cheeks. "I'm starting to get hungry after that description."

"Let's go. And Max will have a treat, too. These are T-bones, so he can enjoy the leftovers."

"He may desert me for you after tonight." Nicholas exited the Tahoe and met her on the sidewalk to her house.

"I'm beginning to change my mind about having a pet. When this is over with, I want a dog. One like Max. I know you mentioned you'd help me, and I might take you up on it. You're the expert on guard dogs." Before she unlocked her door, she shifted toward Nicholas. "We never settled on me going with you to interview my uncle."

He studied her for a few seconds. "He might not be too happy to see me—us. Do you still want to do it?"

"Yes. I owe Erin. She's the one who contacted me first to meet for lunch. I might never have gotten to know her if she hadn't made that first move after my mom's funeral." She grinned. "And since working at the White House, I've discovered diplomacy. I'll persuade my uncle to help us get to the bottom of all this because I know he isn't personally involved." At least she prayed he wasn't. She couldn't dismiss that someone from the Eagleton office had paid Benny Goodwin to keep an eye on who visited Greg. Who? Why, after he was sent to jail?

"Then okay. You can even initiate the contact to set up a time. All right?"

"Yes. Perfect." She unlocked her front door and hurried to turn off the alarm while Max greeted Nicholas. She glanced back at them and some of her wariness of Nicholas's motives faded as she watched her protector playfully roughhousing with his dog.

* * *

"Thank you for seeing me on such short notice, Miss Miller." Nicholas took the seat in front of the desk that Congressman Jeffries's aide gestured toward.

She sat in the one next to him, dressed in an emerald-green pencil skirt, black high heels and a white blouse with cap sleeves. He noticed a matching green jacket hung on a coatrack. Her office wasn't big, but then she was a junior staff member.

"Please, Tabitha." She crossed her long legs. "What brings you to my office?"

"I'm reopening a case and your name came up." He observed her for any reaction to his words, and she didn't let him down. Her pupils dilated. Her body tensed.

"Case? I haven't been involved in any cases."

"It happened two years ago at your apartment complex."

As her forehead crunched, her lower lip stuck out. She brushed back her long, wavy, reddish-blond hair, similar to Erin Eagleton's. "I don't understand."

"Do you recall when Saul Rather, one of Senator Eagleton's interns, was murdered in the parking garage?"

"I wasn't a witness to that murder. I was asleep when it happened, because I remember sirens waking me up. Why do you want to talk with me? I don't know anything about what went down."

He was beginning to wonder if she might know more than she was saying, with the way a defensive wall went up when he mentioned the murder victim. "Did you know Saul Rather?"

"Personally, no. He hadn't lived at the apartment complex but a couple of months, and he kept to himself. I saw him a few times at the Capitol and maybe spoke a handful of words to him. His murderer has already been convicted."

"New evidence has surfaced, and I'm taking a hard look at the case."

"Again, I don't see my connection."

"You and a few of your friends witnessed an argument between Rather and Littleton, the custodian convicted of the crime, the evening before the murder. Do you recall it?"

"Two years ago," she said in a voice full of disbelief. "What do you expect me to remember?"

"What you saw between the two men, your impression of the fight and who else was with you on your balcony."

She blew out a long breath. "No, I mean it was *two* years ago."

"I understand you used to have various aides over to your place after work."

"I used to once a week. Those people would

vary from week to week, so to be able to recall the exact ones at my apartment on that particular day is impossible. The only ones I remember who might have been there are the regulars, although even they didn't come every week."

When she didn't elaborate, Nicholas asked, "Who were they?"

"Sally Young, Becky Wright and Janice Neill. We did a lot of things together back then." Tabitha rose. "I'm sorry I can't be more helpful. Saul Rather had a temper. Word had it, he usually held it together during the workday, but once off work he'd speak his mind. That's all I know."

In his gut, he felt she was holding something back. Nicholas took his time getting to his feet, then slowly lifted his gaze to Tabitha's green eyes, dark with—worry? She came to four inches shorter than he was, so she could have fit into Miss Chick's costume. He knew that was a stretch, and yet she was Congressman Jeffries's aide, had been for several years. Could she be connected to Michael Jeffries's murder case somehow? "One last thing, did you go to the Easter Egg Roll?"

"Yes, along with thousands of others. Congressman Jeffries was there as well as a couple of his staff members. Why? What does that have to do with the murder of Saul Rather?"

"Nothing. Just curious." He thought of the

cufflinks, with the initials *VG* engraved on them, that he found in Margaret Meyer's office. "Was Vincent Geary one of the aides at the event?"

"No. He had some work to finish up on a bill for the congressman." She walked toward the door. "I'm sorry I couldn't have been of more use to you. I need to leave. I have a luncheon scheduled. Duty calls."

He removed his card. "If you can think of anyone who was on the balcony with you that day or possibly would have been, please give me a call."

Out in the main hall of the office building, he lounged against the wall, waiting to see when she would appear to go to her luncheon. Still no Tabitha Miller ten minutes later. His cell phone rang, and he quickly answered the call from Selena.

"Are you backing out of eating lunch at the White House mess with me?" Nicholas asked instead of saying hello.

"Don't you think after spending most of yesterday together we've seen each other enough?"

"Let's not forget this morning at the White House."

"Yes, you're right. You aren't usually far away. I'm calling to let you know my uncle wants to see me for lunch."

"Okay, I'll be at your office in twenty minutes."

"Don't bother. I'm at the Capitol, waiting for Uncle Preston to meet me. He should be here any minute."

He shoved away from the wall, his hand clenching his cell phone. "What happened to *we* would work as a team and talk to him together?"

SIX

"That's why I'm telling you now." Selena moved to a quieter area of the corridor in the Capitol Building while keeping an eye on the exit from the Senate. "I got a call from my uncle's secretary, telling me he can meet with me when the Senate breaks for lunch. I only had twenty minutes to get over here. When I phoned this morning, I didn't think I would get a chance to see Uncle Preston until next week. Unlike you, I'm sharing. Can you get over here?"

"On my way. Where will you two be?"

"The Senate dining room. Do you know where it is? I know it's hard to find. I could ask my uncle to wait for—"

"Yes, I know its location. My grandfather was a senator. Chitchat until I get there."

"Yes, sir. I see my uncle. Talk to you later." She punched the End button and returned her cell to her jacket pocket while the tall, distinguished-looking man with silver hair walked toward her. Imposing. A neutral expression in place. At least her uncle wasn't frowning.

When a colleague intercepted him, Uncle Preston grinned and his face became lively. She sighed, wishing he would respond to her like that. But every time he saw her he saw her mother. She looked so much like her that she was a constant reminder to Uncle Preston of his sister who had blackened the Eagleton name.

"Hi, Selena. Waiting for Senator Eagleton?" Carly Jones, her uncle's chief of staff, asked.

"Yes, we're supposed to have lunch. Do you need to talk to him?"

"Just for a moment about a bill coming up for a vote." Dressed impeccably, with short brown hair, Carly stepped closer and lowered her voice. "I heard there was some trouble at the Easter Egg Roll. I didn't stay long. Too much that needed to be done. What happened?"

"I'm not at liberty to say, but everything has been taken care of." She wasn't going to tell Carly about the break-in and Miss Chick. Her uncle's chief of staff hardly ever talked to her unless she wanted something. Carly was what she called an information gatherer, going from one person to the next to see what she could glean. That might be helpful to her uncle, but Erin had learned to keep her distance and so had Selena.

"I'm glad. I see the senator is free. I won't

keep him long." Carly quickly left to catch Uncle Preston before he reached Selena.

She tried not to stare at Carly and her uncle talking, but something his chief of staff told him didn't make him happy. He was still frowning when he approached Selena.

"Our lunch will be short. I need to talk to another senator before the vote on a bill this afternoon."

"I understand. Do you need to reschedule?" Suddenly she didn't want to talk to her uncle. Growing up listening to her mother talk about him, Selena had become wary of the man by the time she was a teenager. According to her mom, he could be ruthless and cold, and so far, not much she'd witnessed had changed her mind. She hadn't let the thugs in her neighborhood scare her, but Uncle Preston did.

He checked his cell phone then shook his head. "No, I'm tied up for a while, and you said this was important concerning Erin. Let's go in, and I'll ask for a table in a quiet corner. You haven't heard from Erin, have you?" He started down the hallway that led to the dining room.

She understood his desire to find out anything concerning his daughter, but there was a small part of her that wished he'd want to spend time with her because she was his only niece, not because of information she might give him concerning Erin. "No, I wish I had. Nicholas

Cole will be joining us in a few minutes. He's a member of the Capitol K-9 Unit, and we've discovered information that might help Erin."

Her uncle slowed his step. "I'm not a patient man nor do I like surprises."

"I promised Nicholas we would talk to you together."

Silence fell between them until they were seated at a table in front of a large window. He'd informed the staff he was expecting one more person to join him at his table.

"I knew Nicholas Cole's parents and had heard he was working at the White House. I saw him once there. He looks a lot like his father. Are you friends with him?"

Heat seared her cheeks. She rarely blushed, but her uncle got her to. She didn't know her father, and there were times as a child she used to think of Uncle Preston as her father. She even found a photo her mother had and took it to keep. Her mom never missed it. "Yes," she finally answered, realizing she did consider Nicholas a friend. She could talk to him a lot easier than to most people.

"Ah, I see him coming this way."

Selena glanced at Nicholas, strolling under the huge chandelier, its light reflecting off the golden walls. He paused a moment at a table with two senators, shaking their hands and saying a few words before bridging the distance to the table. She knew he came from wealth, but not until she'd seen him in this environment, as though he belonged, did she realize how different their backgrounds were.

Nicholas took the chair near the window, so he faced the diners in the large room. "It's good to see you again, Senator Eagleton."

"I was just telling my niece I knew your parents. And I was a congressman when your grandfather served in the Senate from Maryland. Any interest in going into politics?"

Nicholas picked up a white napkin and placed it in his lap. "I'm enjoying my job and don't see a reason to change."

After the waiter took their orders, her uncle sipped his water then said, "Selena asked me to wait until you arrived to find out why she needed to talk with me. You're here, so why the urgency?"

"We're investigating a lead in Saul Rather's murder."

Uncle Preston's eyebrows hiked up. "Greg Littleton was found guilty. Case closed."

"We're not so sure he's the one who murdered your intern," Selena interjected.

Both men looked at Selena, and she tensed her shoulders. Surprise filled her uncle's face while Nicholas's mouth tightened into a hard line.

Nicholas cleared his throat. "Greg was convicted on circumstantial evidence and some of it has come into question of late. We were at the prison to interview Greg yesterday, and when we left there, someone followed us. We confronted the private detective and discovered you or someone from your office hired him to keep an eye on any people who visit Littleton."

Uncle Preston's forehead furrowed, but he didn't say anything until the waiter set their orders in front of them and left. He stared for a long moment at his poached halibut with saffron nage, then looked Nicholas in the eye. "Who was the private investigator?"

"Benny Goodwin." Nicholas picked up his braised short-rib sandwich and took a bite, watching for any kind of reaction from her uncle.

Popping a sweet-potato fry into her mouth, Selena saw her uncle's jawline harden and his eyes glint. The scent from her crab-cake sandwich churned her stomach.

"First of all, I don't know what this has to do with my daughter. Second, I don't know a Benny Goodwin. I've never used him for any kind of work. If he told you I hired him, he's lying."

"Could someone on your staff have hired Goodwin without your knowledge? When he's paid, it's cash and the private detective has never seen a person associated with the request." Nicholas returned her uncle's intense regard.

"I guess it's possible. I certainly know I don't hire anyone and pay in cash, for accounting reasons. But why would someone from my staff do that?"

"To keep track of what's going on with Littleton because they have something to lose if evidence is uncovered to prove his innocence." Nicholas reached under the white tablecloth and clasped Selena's hand.

She was sure her distress was evident on her face. Her uncle had that effect on her. She wasn't like her mother and had for years wished he would acknowledge that. Her family was small, and she wanted some connection with the few she had. It was lonely being a loner all of her life.

"What does this have to do with Erin? Not that I don't want an innocent man, if he is, exonerated." Uncle Preston shifted his attention from Nicholas to her.

Nicholas squeezed her hand, as if to say she should take this question.

"When Erin went missing, I was determined to find a way to clear her name. I looked into Michael Jeffries's personal life and couldn't find anything that would be a motive for murder. That's when I decided to investigate his professional life. I knew Michael had a couple of current cases he was working on, and I decided to see if anyone connected to those would have a reason to kill him. Erin didn't."

"Of course, my daughter wouldn't," her uncle said in a raised voice, then snapped his mouth closed as a few people glanced their way.

Selena's grip on Nicholas's hand tightened. "Michael and she were good friends, and she never indicated any problems between them to me. If nothing jumped out with the current cases, I was going to work back from there. Littleton's case was badly handled by his court-appointed attorney. The more I dug into the evidence, the more I'd come to believe, like Michael, that he was innocent."

Uncle Preston's stern expression relaxed, and slowly his features transformed into a pleasant look. "You never said anything to me about that or sought my help," he said to Selena, as though surprised by that fact.

She released Nicholas's grasp and straightened in her chair, her gaze fixed on her uncle. "You'd made it clear you didn't really consider me a member of your family, but Erin accepted me from the beginning."

His eyes, so like Erin's, flared. "I deserved that." He blew out a long breath. "Not knowing if my daughter is alive or not has made me take a good hard look at myself. I've been pushing the police to discover the truth, even hired my investigators, but you went out and did something yourself. I haven't been the father I should have been…or the uncle to you."

Selena dug her teeth into her lower lip to keep her jaw from dropping.

"I've been reconsidering how I treated you the last couple of months, so when you called me to ask for a meeting, I rearranged my schedule to see you right away. I could have asked you for any news you had about Erin over the phone. I knew I couldn't put off telling you how I felt, and I wasn't going to do that by phone. My stubbornness has kept me from forgiving your mother, and she is dead. I could never condone her lifestyle, but she was my only sibling. I should have been better than what I was."

Selena blinked the tears away. She wouldn't cry in front of her uncle or Nicholas. She'd learned when she was young to hide her real emotions. "I didn't condone my mother's lifestyle, either. I left home as soon as I could. I couldn't help her if she wouldn't help herself." She stared at her uneaten sandwich. This conversation had thrown her past front and center. Foremost, she regretted that there was nothing she could have done to help her mother and now it was too late.

"I'm sorry. You should have felt you could come to me. I cut you off as though you were your mother, and now I have a daughter running away from the authorities when all your mother did was make a social spectacle of herself."

Nicholas cleared his throat, drawing their attention to him. "Should I leave?"

She said, "No," immediately, with Uncle Preston's two seconds behind hers.

Her uncle checked his watch, flashing her a smile. "Let's eat. They serve good food here." He cut into his halibut. "And if I can help either one of you in this Littleton case or anything else that can prove my daughter innocent, I will."

As Selena took her first bite of her crab-cake sandwich, she couldn't believe how well this conversation had gone. She'd prayed to the Lord to help her concerning her uncle, and she'd finally received an answer. *Maybe You* are *listening to me. Thank You, God.*

Nicholas escorted Selena back to the White House after their luncheon with Senator Eagleton. "Do you think he's telling the truth? Do you think he's had contact with Erin in any way?"

Selena tossed her purse on the desk in her office then swung around toward Nicholas. "We don't, as you heard, have a close relationship, but I think he is telling the truth. Erin wouldn't put her father at risk. She was always conscious of his political career. Before all this happened, there had been talk of him running for president. Now I doubt he will." She propped herself against her desk and grasped its edge. "What did Tabitha Miller have to say when you interviewed her?"

"She couldn't remember much about the day Littleton and Rather argued by the pool or which congressional aides were on her balcony with her. In other words, she was a dead end."

"Did you believe her?"

"I don't know." He kneaded the side of his neck. "Not so much about not remembering specifics about the day or people, but when I asked her how well she'd known Saul Rather, she said hardly at all. Yet there was something in her body language that made me doubt her. For just a second she touched her nose and averted her gaze."

"I don't remember any gossip about her from two years ago, but I do know she flits from one man to the next. Anyone who can better her standing in Washington. I think I even heard some chatter about her going after Michael. But you know how reliable rumors can be."

"There could be truth in that one. I'll do some checking." Nicholas closed the distance between them.

"More likely she saw Michael as a way to elevate her position on the congressman's staff. That doesn't mean Michael went along with that."

"I'm glad the senator gave us permission to investigate his staff members to see if we can find anyone who would have hired Goodwin. What I wish I could really do is access their financial records, but we don't have enough for a warrant at this time. Maybe later."

"Follow the money trail?"

"It often pays off." He locked gazes with her, being drawn even nearer by the glittering blue of her eyes. Listening earlier to the senator talking to Selena about their nonexistent relationship, he'd caught regret and vulnerability in her eyes. He'd been in the same situation with his parents, wanting a relationship that never materialized. He prayed Selena and her uncle could repair their familial bond. "What are you doing this afternoon?"

"I have several meetings. One of those with the president. How about you?"

Her spicy scent surrounded him, roping him to her. He inched forward. "Interviewing a suspect concerning the break-in of General Meyer's office."

"I'd ask who but I know you. Mum's the word."

"We have a few leads from going through the security videos, nothing solid, but that doesn't mean we won't narrow the suspect list down to a few."

"And then keep an eye on them," she said with a grin.

His heartbeat began tapping faster against

his rib cage. She had a great smile. "I'll make a law-enforcement officer out of you before this is over." He couldn't resist plunging his fingers into the thick waves of her hair.

Her eyelids slid partially closed, and she shivered. "Not me. You can have the job. Look what has happened with my one attempt at investigating."

Holding her head framed between his hands, he leaned toward her until he was a breath away. "True. You'd better leave that to me." Then he brushed his lips across hers, lightly, teasingly.

Now his heartbeat hammered maddeningly within his chest. The urge to sweep her against him and deepen the kiss overwhelmed him. He started to, when a rap at the door echoed through his hazy thoughts.

Selena reacted by pushing away from the desk, stepping to the side and breaking their contact, her hair mussed where he'd held her. She started for the door.

"Wait."

She turned toward him, and he ran his fingers through her strands to neaten them.

"There. I wouldn't want any tongues wagging around here about us. I'll let the person in on my way out." He winked and sauntered toward the door. "See you later today."

He peered over his shoulder as she greeted

one of the president's staff. He wanted to kiss her properly. He'd choose a better place next time.

Earlier today, he'd found out when Vincent Geary would be in his office this afternoon. He intended to have a talk with him about the gold cufflink he'd found in General Meyer's office the day of the Easter Egg Roll. He'd discovered they had been purchased at a Washington, DC, jeweler last Christmas by the congressman as a gift to each of his male staff members. Jeffries's aide had been dodging his calls and attempts to interview him. He was determined Geary wouldn't today.

Twenty minutes later, he sat across from the congressman's aide in his office. "I'm glad you could meet with me on short notice." He intentionally hadn't set up an appointment with Geary after the two times he'd tried and been given the runaround.

The tall, slender, dark-haired aide with equally dark brown eyes lounged back in his chair, his elbows resting on the arms while his fingers formed a steeple. "What can I do for you? Is this something to do with Congressman Jeffries's son's murder? I'd love to tell him that you are close to arresting someone. Erin Eagleton, perhaps."

"This concerns something different. General Meyer discovered someone had rifled through her files the morning of the Easter Egg Roll."

His eyebrows beetled together. "How can I help you?"

"After the break-in, one of your cufflinks was found under the general's console behind her desk." He'd taken a photo of the piece of evidence and gave his cell phone to Geary. "Is that yours?"

"It looks like it."

"You hadn't been on her calendar that day or the day before. How did your cufflink get there?" Nicholas scrutinized him for any small indication he wasn't speaking the truth—not that his gut feeling would ever hold up in court.

"I have no idea unless it's been there since the last time I met with the general in her office, which was last week. Later that day, I noticed I'd lost it."

"And you didn't backtrack and check to see if someone found it? I understand it was a special gift from the congressman."

"No. I'd been quite a few places that day."

Although Geary's expression seemed relaxed, when Nicholas had first mentioned the cufflink, his left eye had twitched twice and his mouth had tensed slightly before Geary maintained control over his reactions. Smooth. "Did you say anything to anyone about losing it?"

"I had a dinner meeting with the congressman. I might have said something to him. If it was under a console, the cleaning staff could easily have overlooked it. Will I be able to get it back?"

"When the investigation is over."

Geary frowned. "I've missed wearing them. I suppose I should be glad that at least you found the missing one, and I'll get it back sometime in the future."

Nicholas started to rise but stopped. "Oh, by the way, why were you at the White House the evening before the Easter Egg Roll? In the West Wing." Geary had been one of many caught on camera near the general's office.

The aide's mouth firmed into a scowl. "I attended a reception with the congressman in the Roosevelt Room before the state dinner. I've done nothing wrong and resent the accusation."

"What accusation?"

Geary glared at him but remained silent.

Nicholas stood and extended his hand for Geary to shake. He finally did and the clammy feeling confirmed to him that the aide had been lying. But he didn't have any hard evidence to prove it—just years learning to read people.

Geary accompanied him into the hallway and Nicholas felt the aide's eyes on him as he strode toward the elevator. When the doors swished open, Congressman Harland Jeffries exited. With his hair graying, his tanned features stood out even more.

He spied Nicholas and said, "Weren't you here earlier today?"

"Yes, sir." Nicholas shook the man's cold hand. "I needed to see Vincent Geary. He mentioned losing one of his initialed cufflinks that you gave him at Christmas. He felt bad about losing it."

The congressman looked at a spot behind Nicholas. "It seems I remember him telling me he lost one somewhere."

"When?"

"Frankly, everything has been a blur for me with all that has happened. I don't remember exactly."

The elevator doors opened with the down arrow lit up. "Thanks, Congressman." Nicholas stepped inside and punched the button for the lobby. His gut instinct told him Jeffries was hiding something.

When he headed out of the building, his cell phone rang. He saw it was his captain, so he found a quiet area to answer the call. "What's going on, Gavin?"

"A woman who reportedly looks like Erin Eagleton was spotted spying on Congressman Jeffries's house. I need you and Isaac Black to go check it out."

For Selena's sake, Nicholas hoped it *was* Erin—it meant her cousin was alive. But finding Erin would also mean bringing her in for questioning and grilling her about the night of Michael Jeffries's murder. Was Erin the killer?

Nicholas pulled up in front of Congressman Jeffries's mansion, parking behind Isaac Black, a Capitol K-9 Unit member who used to work for the CIA. With Max on a leash, Nicholas approached Isaac, a tall, muscular guy with dark brown hair and eyes. Abby, his canine partner and a beagle, wagged her tail and greeted Max.

Nicholas scanned the large home. "I understand from Gavin that a neighbor, Mrs. Applegate, reported a woman who fit Erin's description was outside the congressman's house, looking in the windows. Jeffries is at the Capitol and is aware that we're going to search the grounds. He mentioned his gardener works today and may have seen something."

"I'll interview the gardener while you talk to the neighbor. I'm going to do a walk-around and see if I can find him."

"I will, too, after I talk with Mrs. Applegate. Are you having Abby sniff for a bomb?"

"As a precaution." Isaac glanced around. "If it was Erin skulking around, why would she come here? For what purpose?"

"I don't know. And we don't know if it *is* Erin. I agree we take every precaution and check everything out. We don't need the congressman killed, too."

With Max beside him, Nicholas made his way to the palatial house to the right of the Jeffries's mansion. A petite woman with graying hair, dressed in jeans, a blue shirt and straw hat, opened the door. "I'm here to see Mrs. Applegate."

"I'm she. Please come in, Officer."

"Max is my K-9 partner. He is very well behaved. May I bring him in?"

"Of course. I love dogs."

Mrs. Applegate led them to the living room. Nicholas sat in a wingback, while she sat across from him on a couch. The casually dressed lady was in stark contrast to the elegant surroundings. "Please tell me what you saw earlier. You reported seeing a woman trespassing on Congressman Jeffries's property at around two o'clock."

"Yes. I don't wear a watch when I work in my gardens, but I'd just gone back out after a short break to work on my roses, my prize flowers. If you come back in three or four weeks, they'll take your breath away."

"What I saw of your flower beds is beautiful."

Mrs. Applegate beamed. "Any artist loves to hear that. Anyway, I was outside working when I saw a woman in glamorous, big black sunglasses, just like Erin always wore, looking in a window of the congressman's house. She had a silk scarf wrapped around her head like from an old Grace Kelly movie. I assumed it was Erin because the few times I saw Michael and Erin arriving at the congressman's house in a convertible, Erin wore a scarf just like that to protect her beautiful, long curly hair. Anyway, she didn't look like anyone he has working for him. I'm familiar with his staff and gardeners."

"How tall do you think she was?"

"Five-seven, five-eight."

Nicholas knew from previous meetings with the Capitol K-9 Unit that Erin Eagleton was five feet eight inches tall. Forensics had noted that the murderer was, too.

"Of course, I can't be certain it was Erin Eagleton, but I know from watching the news that she's been missing ever since Michael was killed, so I called it in immediately." Mrs. Applegate shook her head. "Such a tragedy about Michael. I was on vacation in Paris when the murder occurred."

"You said she was wearing sunglasses, but did you get a look at her face, features such as her nose and mouth?"

"I only got a brief glance at her face, and I didn't have my eyeglasses on, but because of the sunglasses, scarf and her general height and build, I thought the person was Erin."

Nicholas nodded. "What did you see the woman do?"

"She ducked down when the gardener came

around the side of the house, then hurried away, running off in the opposite direction."

"Will you come outside and show me exactly?"

"I thought you might say that. I'm ready to go. Anything to help Harland. Poor man. Losing his son like that. Harland is always checking on me, especially if he hasn't seen me in my gardens in several days."

As they walked from the house and around the side toward Jeffries's property, she told Nicholas stories of how much the congressman had helped her. Nicholas had to admit that the man was a study in contradictions. Kind to some, like his captain. Jeffries had even started a foster home on his property. But that didn't mean the congressman wasn't corrupt. Nicholas kept thinking about Jeffries's ties to Thorn Industries, a shady pharmaceutical company that he'd said had tried to strong-arm him with bribes he refused to take. Nicholas wasn't so sure Jeffries hadn't taken those bribes. But again, he couldn't prove anything. Without proof, his captain didn't want to hear a word against Jeffries.

Mrs. Applegate stopped near her rosebushes, which were beginning to leaf out. She pointed to a large window on the right side of the mansion with bushes under it. "That's where I saw her. You know, now that I think about it the woman looks similar in style and build to Tabitha Miller, too—she's one of Harland's aides—but there wouldn't be any reason for her to be skulking around the congressman's house."

He envisioned the woman he'd interviewed earlier today. She was around Erin's height and had that same glamorous style as Erin. Nicholas could easily imagine her in huge black sunglasses and a silk scarf keeping her hair from being blown around in a convertible. Could Tabitha be the woman Mrs. Applegate had seen? Mrs. Applegate was right when she said Tabitha wouldn't have a reason to sneak around. The congressman's staff would admit her inside.

No, it made more sense that it was Erin. But why had she come? What was she looking for?

A few minutes before seven, the last of the meetings over, Selena was ready to go home. Nicholas had left a text telling her he was going to Congressman Jeffries's house and might be a while before he was finished. All she wanted to do was go home and collapse. Halfway through her second meeting she'd felt all the exhaustion from the past weeks' frantic pace physically and emotionally catching up with her. Her two days of rest hadn't turned into any rest at all, not with the break-in at her home and the visit to the prison.

She gathered her purse and work tablet and headed for the underground parking lot. As she strolled toward her car at the far end, she thought of all the things she needed to do.

Her cell phone chimed. Nicholas. "Are you done for the day?" she asked him.

"Yes, I've left the congressman's house. Are you heading home?"

"I'm nearly at my car."

"You need to wait for me. Remember, I follow you to and from work."

"I fell asleep at my desk. I imagined my bed and thought that might be a better place to sleep. I'm going to have to finish some work at home. I don't usually do that."

"I'm not far from the White House. Wait. I'll feel better."

"Okay," she said and gave him her precise location. Nicholas said something, but she couldn't hear over the sound of a motorcycle behind her and heading toward the exit. She raised her voice. "I didn't hear you. Just a sec until the bike passes." She twisted toward the motorcycle.

All Selena saw was a person dressed totally in black, closer than she realized. The biker slowed to a stop and reached out toward her, snatching her work tablet.

"Don't." She lunged toward her attacker to grab the tablet back.

There was a flash of metal, then something sharp cut into her arm. She was knocked back against a car behind her. Slamming into its bumper, the air swooshing from her lungs, she sank to the pavement as the biker revved the engine.

SEVEN

The sound of a motorcycle, Selena crying out "Don't!" and a thud chilled Nicholas to the core. He pressed down on the accelerator. "Selena. Selena, are you okay? What happened?" he shouted, sure she'd dropped her cell phone.

The seconds ticked by agonizingly slow.

Then Selena came on the line. "I was attacked...and stabbed—"

"Are you hurt?"

"My arm's bleeding."

His heartbeat pounded. "Listen to me. I'm calling Security. I'm four minutes away." He turned on his siren, "Make that two minutes."

He called Security, giving details of where Selena had been attacked and asking them to shut down the exit from there and send medical help. Now he was only sixty seconds away. He approached the tunnel to the underground parking, his heartbeat thundering in his ears. He saw a black motorcycle speeding past him, its driver dressed in black, and wanted to give chase. He'd heard what sounded like a motorcycle in the background when talking to Selena, but he didn't know if that was the assailant on the bike. Looking through the rearview mirror, he called local police and reported the license number, though, and where it was headed.

He was the first on the scene, parking his SUV near Selena and hopping from his car. She sat against a vehicle's bumper, looking dazed, a stream of blood oozing between her fingers clasped over the wound. It ran down her arm. As he rounded the front of his Tahoe, several White House security officers jogged toward them.

She looked at him as he knelt next to her. "Selena?"

"I'm okay...a little stunned. Black motorcycle," she said, trying to take a breath. "Rider all in black." That was all she could get out before needing to close her eyes for a moment.

If only I'd gone after the bike, Nicholas thought. But getting to Selena had been more important. "He passed me on the way in—I called in the police. Medical help is on the way."

She glanced at her arm. "No ambulance...just need...stitches."

She spoke almost as though she had disassociated herself from the incident, but she was having trouble forming sentences. "Did you hit your head again?"

"No. Just had the—" she blinked "—breath knocked out of me." She inhaled deeply. "No—cracked ribs."

"Don't move. I'm talking to the officers then I'll be right back."

Before he stood, she added, "He took my… work tablet."

"I'll let security know."

Please let her be okay, he thought as adrenaline had him moving when all he wanted was to stay by her side.

Selena felt shell-shocked more than anything. Her arm barely hurt, but she saw the blood coursing down it in spite of clasping the wound. While Nicholas spoke with the three men in a low voice, she tried to think of something in her car she could use to stop the bleeding. Her mind refused to function properly. She couldn't string a coherent thought together. Probably blood loss affecting her.

One of the men, trained as a paramedic, stooped next to her with a first-aid kit and began working on her wound while Nicholas pointed toward the exit. He moved to a knife on the pavement and instructed an officer to bag it. She'd felt the cut but hadn't seen the knife, just a flash of metal.

After that, Nicholas strode to his SUV and released Max. While a bandage was being wrapped around her arm, Max sniffed the air and set off, following a trail from the direction the motorcycle had come from.

She began to tremble, chills streaking through her. Pain finally leaked into her mind, demanding attention.

Watching Max come to a stop at a narrow parking spot in the underground garage, Nicholas noted the space would easily fit a motorcycle.

He gave Max a treat. "Good boy. Now all I need to figure out is whose bike was here. Looks like more security video for me." He tried to think of White House staffers who rode a motorcycle to work. He'd get a list and start questioning them. They usually knew who else was a biker. He checked the camera; the area wasn't in direct line of sight but the approach was. He would find the owner if the local police hadn't caught him already.

His priority now was to get Selena to the ER to have her wound taken care of and to make sure she wasn't injured anywhere else. Adrenaline could be masking something else.

He and Max jogged back to the crime scene. The paramedic-trained security officer had finished bandaging her. Still sitting on the pavement, she turned her head slightly and looked right at him. There was an ashen cast to her skin and she shook. As he neared her, he noticed the pool of blood next to her as though a vein had been cut.

"Open my passenger door," Nicholas said to the paramedic working on Selena. "I'm taking her to the emergency room."

Nicholas squatted next to her and lifted her into his arms. Cradled against him, she gave him a weak smile. He carried her to his Tahoe and settled her onto the front passenger seat.

"Thanks," she said to the paramedic then Nicholas while supporting her arm against her trembling body. Shock was setting in.

Nicholas leaned over and buckled her in then took off his jacket and covered her. Selena reclined back and shut her eyes. "Hold on. It won't be long." As he rounded the back of the Tahoe and put Max inside, he motioned to another White House security officer. "Take care of the crime scene, and notify Dan Calvert about what happened and that Miss Barrow's work tablet was stolen. Put a rush on the knife. I want to know if there are any fingerprints on it."

"Will do."

The security officer with paramedic training looked at Selena then back at Nicholas. "She'll be all right once she gets stitches."

"Thanks for taking care of her."

He hurried around the driver's side, slid behind the wheel and started the engine. As he went over a speed bump, he glanced at Selena and found her gaze glued on him.

"Okay?" he asked as he slipped into the flow of traffic.

"I'll live."

"You scared me back there. Do you remember anything about your attacker?"

"It happened so fast. I'm starting to get my bearings."

"Good. You need around-the-clock protection."

"You can't do that and continue to work."

"Yes, I can, especially when General Meyer hears."

Selena drew in a deep breath "I'm planning another event for the president. I don't have time to take off. He just told me about it today."

"I see you're beginning to feel more like yourself. Arguing every detail with me."

"I'm not arguing. Pointing out the hurdles in your plan. I want you to find the person who took my tablet. I assume the Miss Chick impostor, the person who ransacked my house and the motorcyclist are the same person."

"Agreed. What was on the tablet?"

"Information pertaining to my job. For instance, most of the plans for the Easter Egg Roll. So I need you working."

"And I need you alive." As he spoke, he

realized how important Selena was becoming to the case—to him.

As he pulled into the ER, he decided he would talk with the captain about this. He needed another team member to help him. He felt this was all tied to the Jeffries case. *If we find who's after Selena, we may be apprehending Jeffries's murderer.*

Spending most of the night in the ER wasn't Selena's idea of fun, but finally Nicholas pulled into her driveway as dawn began to pinken the sky. She yawned.

"You need to get some rest." Nicholas opened his door. "Stay there. I'll help you."

She ignored his instruction and climbed from the Tahoe as he came to the passenger side, frowning. "I tolerated you carrying me to the car at the crime scene and at the ER, but I caught a catnap on the way here and I'm fine." Actually, she did more than tolerate it. She cherished the strong feel of his arms around her because for a brief moment in the garage, she realized how close she'd come to being seriously injured.

"Twenty minutes isn't sufficient sleep." Nicholas released Max from the back of the Tahoe.

"About my Mustang. You should have driven me there to pick it up."

"Not until you've rested like the ER doc said.

You lost quite a bit of blood last night. Max was worried."

She chuckled. "But not you?"

"Yeah, me, too."

Selena paused and bent to pet Max. "I'll be good as new by tomorrow, boy. Will you tell your partner that?"

Max barked.

She straightened too quickly. The action of leaning over caused the yard to spin. She closed her eyes and got her bearings before she climbed the porch steps. When she looked at Nicholas beside her, she knew he hadn't missed her bout of light-headedness. Slow and easy or he would declare her an invalid. And she did need that sleep.

Inside the house, she placed her purse on the table by the door. Before she went to bed, however, she wanted to know what he'd discovered about her assault. "You haven't said anything about what happened last night. What does White House Security know?"

"There were a couple of fingerprints on the kitchen knife used in the attack. One that they could match."

"Who?"

"Vincent Geary."

"Why would he be interested in the Littleton case? That's what the assault has to be about. This all started when I began digging into it."

"Good question and one I will be asking him. I'm having him brought to headquarters for me to interview."

She whistled. "You mean business bringing him in."

"I want to take him out of his comfort zone."

She thought back to the scene in the underground garage. "I think the biker had on black gloves."

"I still need to know why Geary's fingerprints are on the knife."

"So when will you be leaving?" She started for the stairs.

"As soon as my replacement arrives."

Stopping, she glanced over her shoulder. "Who?"

"Brooke Clark. She's a fellow Capitol K-9 Unit member."

"Couldn't you just leave Max? He's great company."

"I called my captain last night, and he'd already heard from General Meyer. You are to have protection. That comes from the president and Senator Eagleton."

"My uncle?" She slowly rotated toward Nicholas, who covered the space between them.

"Yes. They were both at the same gathering last night, and when they heard about the attack, they insisted you be protected, especially after what happened at the Easter Egg Roll. The president was not happy about your office and the general's being compromised. I have a feeling heads will be rolling if we don't come up with answers. Soon. That's from the general and the head of the Secret Service. Someone in our midst isn't playing nice."

"My body can attest to that. No cracked ribs, but I'm going to have bruises. In the past week, I've had more physical contact than when I was growing up with gangs all around."

His eyes twinkled, and one corner of his mouth lifted. "Are you sure I can't help you up the stairs?"

"I'm not even going to answer that."

As she mounted the steps, Nicholas's chuckles floated to her. If she was truthful with herself, she was glad for the protection. That thought took her by surprise. She would never have admitted that in the past. What was it about Nicholas that made her so easily persuaded?

"I'm being framed. First the incident with General Meyer's office and now this." Vincent Geary's face reddened with anger, one hand clenched on the table in the interview room at headquarters.

Nicholas took the chair next to Geary, not the one across from him. He wanted to invade this man's space, make him squirm. "Then explain your fingerprints on this kitchen knife."

He held up the evidence bag with it inside, its carved ivory handle distinctive.

Geary's eyes widened. "My fingerprints are on it because it's mine. I have a whole set of them on my kitchen counter. Where was this found?"

"In the underground parking garage at the White House. Used in an attack on Selena Barrow."

"The tour director?"

"Yes, and the president has taken a personal interest in this situation."

The red flushed from the aide's face. "When did the attack happen?"

"Last night at seven. An assailant riding a black motorcycle snatched her tablet from her and stabbed her then fled. The bike was found this morning and your fingerprints were on the gas tank and side of the seat."

Geary's mouth dropped open. "That's impossible. I have an alibi."

"What is it?"

"I was meeting with Congressman Jeffries and several other members of Congress, including White and Langford, at his house."

Nicholas slid a pad toward him. "Write their names down, and I'll check it out."

"I've never ridden a motorcycle."

Nicholas rose. "If you want to prove that without any doubt, I would suggest you hand me your cell phone until I return. I wouldn't want you to call your boss and get him to vouch for you."

Anger flooded his face again. Geary dug into his pocket and slapped the cell phone into Nicholas's outstretched hand. "Congressman Jeffries is above reproach. He has a stellar reputation."

"Anyway," he said, hardly agreeing with that assessment, "it's not easy to dispute fingerprint evidence."

"I don't know how, but someone planted those fingerprints."

Nicholas exited the interview room and headed for his Tahoe, making a call to Brooke Clark to see how things were going at Selena's. He hoped she was still asleep. "Anything happening there?"

"The grass has grown a millimeter since you left an hour ago." Laughter filled Brooke's light voice.

"Funny. Is Selena still asleep?"

"Yes. Do you want me to call you when she wakes up?"

He could still hear the smirk in her words. "No. Just keep her safe, but don't tell her I said that."

The next call he made was a carefully worded one to Congressman Jeffries's home; a butler assured Nicholas that Harland was home. Then Nicholas texted Isaac Black, asking his fellow

K-9 Unit member to immediately interview Senator Langford to verify Geary's alibi. Isaac texted back that he was on his way.

As Nicholas drove to Jeffries's home, he thought about the case. The problem was that whoever was behind this was a frequent visitor to the White House or someone who worked there, because it wasn't easy to get inside otherwise and know the layout so well to go undetected.

When he was admitted into the congressman's study, Harland Jeffries was sitting on a couch reading a book.

He peered at Nicholas. "Come in. I hope you've found the woman who was lurking around my house earlier. Clare Applegate was very concerned for me."

"Yes, she was." Nicholas took the seat across from Jeffries. "Did you find anything missing, disturbed inside or outside?"

"Not that I or my staff can tell." Jeffries closed his book and laid it on the end table next to him.

"I understand you've had cameras installed outside since Michael's murder. Was anything suspicious on them?"

"Yes, the woman was caught on tape, but I couldn't see her face."

"Like she knew the cameras were there?"

"Yes."

"Who knew about them?"

"The security company who put them in and my staff. It wasn't a secret but not a well-known fact, either."

Nicholas relaxed back in the overstuffed chair. "Are you aware that I talked with Vincent Geary yesterday in connection with the break-in of General Meyer's office?"

"Yes, and I already protested to the general. He would have no reason to do that. I understand his cufflink was found at the scene. Someone could have placed it there anytime or he lost it when he was in the office on business for me."

"He was brought in today for questioning in another matter that occurred yesterday. Selena Barrow was assaulted in the underground parking garage at the White House when she was leaving work."

The congressman frowned. "What time?"

"Seven last night. Geary's fingerprints were found on the weapon, as well as the motorcycle used during the attack."

His frown evolved into a furious expression. "What's going on here? There's no way he could have been in two places at the same time. He was here at seven and didn't leave until nine. The culprit can't be him."

"How do you explain the fingerprints?"

"Someone stole the weapon from his house."

"On the motorcycle?"

The congressman waved his hand in the air.

"I don't know. It's your job to figure it out. He's being framed. You need to be out there looking for the real assailant. If you don't want to take my word, check with Congressman White and Senator Langford about Geary's alibi. They'll tell you the same thing."

"We are right now. Do you know anyone on your staff that might do this? You said yourself your staff knew about the additional cameras outside."

"I can't imagine anyone on… Wait, Tabitha Miller has been calling in sick a lot lately. In fact, she left work yesterday afternoon and didn't attend the meeting last night at my house. She said she was getting sick." Jeffries rubbed his nape. "I don't know. She probably was, but she's been acting strangely the past couple of months."

Tabitha's name sure came up a lot in this investigation. Nicholas stood. "I appreciate you taking your time to discuss this."

The congressman shoved to his feet and walked with Nicholas to the front door. "Of course. I don't want to see a good man's name damaged for something he didn't do. I understand you feel the same way. I heard you're looking into the Littleton case. I'm glad. My son was working on that and believed him innocent."

"I only want the guilty to go to prison."

As he strode to the Tahoe, he glanced back

and saw Jeffries looking at him out the window. The congressman said the right words, but Nicholas couldn't bring himself to trust everything he said. Call it a gut feeling, but he couldn't shake it. He slipped into his SUV. Now to talk to Congressman White.

Her throbbing arm dragged Selena from her dream of lying on a beach reading a book as the sun blanketed her in warmth. When she opened her eyes to her bedroom, reality washed over her, especially when she touched the white bandage around her left forearm. She glanced at the bedside clock. She'd slept for three hours. Her stomach rumbled its hunger.

Slowly she rose and descended the stairs to the first floor, wondering if Nicholas was back from talking with Vincent Geary. She couldn't understand Geary being behind the attack unless he was somehow involved in the Littleton case. She'd only talked with him on a few occasions.

At the bottom of the steps, she peered into the living room and spied a strange dog—a beautiful golden retriever, lying on her floor. A petite woman with short dark hair and blue eyes, carrying a mug, came around the corner from the kitchen.

She smiled. "I'm Brooke Clark, babysitter extraordinaire."

The laughter in her gaze enticed Selena to grin and reply, "I'm Selena Barrow, but then you already knew that. I could say I'm a victim extraordinaire, but I'm not owning up to that title."

"Would you like coffee? I took the liberty of making some."

"Sure, but even more, I want something to eat. How about you?"

"Starving. I was thinking of sending Mercy on a rescue trip to the nearest fast-food joint."

As she followed Brooke into the kitchen, Selena peered back at Mercy, who had perked up at the mention of her name. "She's beautiful. What's her specialty?"

"Retrieving."

"That makes sense given her breed." Selena opened the refrigerator door. "I have the makings of a turkey-and-cheese sandwich."

"Sounds great. Nicholas called not too long ago to say he's on his way back here."

"I'll make him a sandwich, too, and if he doesn't eat it, we can split it. I'm hungry enough. I haven't eaten in almost twenty-four hours."

Five minutes later, Selena gave Brooke a plate with her lunch then took a seat next to her at the kitchen table. "Did he say anything about the case?"

"It looks like Vincent Geary is innocent. He has an airtight alibi."

"But the fingerprints?"

"Not his. They were planted in both places. Fingerprints can be transferred, and there's evidence of that occurring when they were closely analyzed."

"Why would someone frame him?"

Brooke shrugged. "If we knew, we'd probably know who was behind the attack."

"Do you think the assailant is also Michael's killer?" Selena picked up a potato chip and popped it into her mouth.

"It would be great to solve both cases."

"And Erin could come home." *If she's alive.* She wished she knew for sure her cousin was alive even if she only saw her from afar.

"Nicholas said you believe Erin is innocent."

"She's family and I know her. She wouldn't kill Michael. Like Vincent being framed for my assault, things might not appear as they really are."

"True. I've seen that in other cases."

"What's Nicholas like at work?" The grin on Brooke's face made Selena want to take back the question. "Forget I asked that. I've seen him on the job at the White House. He's thorough and intuitive."

"He doesn't take anything at face value. That's why when Vincent Geary insisted he was innocent, he had the lab go back and analyze the fingerprints under a microscope, a more thorough analysis."

So Nicholas was the right law-enforcement officer to help her prove her cousin wasn't guilty. At least it sounded as if he had an open mind. He did with Littleton. That gave her hope. "I'm grateful he's been around lately."

"He's a good guy to have on your side."

She was beginning to see that, even though years ago she'd promised herself she would stand on her own two feet—be totally independent. She saw what happened to her mother, and she didn't want to go down that road. Ever. Her drinking and constant need for love from the wrong men had driven her to an early death. It saddened her because her mom had had such potential at one time.

Chimes echoed through the house. Selena started to rise to answer the front door, when Brooke hopped to her feet and said, "Stay here. You shouldn't go."

Selena stood, her body taut. When Brooke let Nicholas into the house, Selena leaned against the edge of the table, releasing the tension. Brooke and Nicholas talked in low voices.

"Okay, you two. If it's about my case, I'd like to know what's happening. I was the one attacked. Remember?"

Nicholas lifted his head and snagged her with an intense gaze, his expression grim. "I was telling Brooke that we're back to square one since I've ruled out Vincent Geary."

Brooke turned toward Selena. "I insisted on coming back tonight since Nicholas hasn't gotten any sleep. I'm reminding him that he can't stand guard twenty-four hours without consequences."

Selena straightened and folded her arms over her chest. "I agree. In fact, I insist. I can always complain to General Meyer."

Nicholas scowled. "Going over my head won't win points with me."

Selena laughed, the action shedding what stress she had left. "Brooke, I like your suggestion. One person can't do it all." She zeroed in on Nicholas. "You need to sleep without worrying about protecting me."

"Good. I'm glad we got that settled." Brooke called Mercy. "We're leaving, but I'll be back at nine. I have a dinner date with my guy." Her face lit with a huge grin.

"If you need to, come a bit later." Nicholas opened the door for his team member. "I don't want to interrupt your plans."

"Jonas will understand. And tomorrow morning, I'd better not see you until nine. The captain said we're to work together."

Selena sat as Nicholas locked the door after Brooke and Mercy left. "I'm going to church tomorrow at ten. This is my Sunday to help with coffee hour after the service." She gestured toward a plate. "I made you a sandwich."

He joined her at the table with Max lying on the floor between their chairs. "Tell me what happened this morning."

As he ate, Nicholas recalled the interview with Vincent then told her about checking the aide's alibi. "I'm not convinced Vincent isn't messed up in the Jeffries case somehow."

"What do you think of Harland Jeffries? I know my uncle isn't a fan of his. They've been political rivals through the years."

"I'm not a big fan of Jeffries, either."

Reaching for her coffee mug, Selena stopped in midmotion. "Why aren't you? He has a long list of public service. He's actively involved in All Our Kids foster home."

"Speaking of the home, Max and I usually volunteer on Sunday afternoons. Would you mind going with us tomorrow? If not, I can cancel this week."

"No, don't. I love kids. I'm involved through my church with various activities when my schedule allows."

"Max enjoys the children, too. That's when he gets to play. All service dogs need playtime. So much is asked of them when they're on duty."

She sipped her coffee, watching Nicholas finishing his sandwich. "You look tired."

"Going a night without sleep is no big deal. When I was a Navy SEAL and on assignment, sometimes I had to catch sleep whenever and wherever I could. Once I slept on a rocky ledge halfway up a mountain. One wrong move and I'd have been dead in the ravine."

"You can take a nap. Max will protect me. That and my gun."

"No. If I sleep now, it will throw me off for tonight. Brooke is right about taking shifts, and then on Monday I can work the case while you're at the White House, if you promise not to leave the West Wing without me."

"I promise, after what happened in the parking garage." She covered his hand on the table between them. "Thank you for being there so quickly. I think if I hadn't turned and stepped back, the motorcycle would have run me down. Several of the staff members have bikes, and I didn't think anything of it when I heard it coming."

"Then why did you turn?" He clasped her hand between both of his.

"I don't know. A gut feeling. I just did." Either way, she thanked God she had. "Let's not discuss the case tomorrow. Give ourselves a day of relaxation with the children."

"That sounds like a good game plan. I sometimes do my best detecting when I'm not focused on it."

He pushed to his feet and drew her up against him with his arms entwined around her. Her pulse rate accelerated. Every time she got close to Nicholas her feelings shifted inside her. After seeing her mother go through man after man, she'd vowed to remain single. She didn't want to repeat any of her mom's mistakes. So much heartache. She'd had enough in her childhood to last her a lifetime.

And yet, when Nicholas framed her face between his large hands, she melted into him, her legs quivering. She tightened her uninjured arm about him and peered up at him. A golden light twinkled in his brown eyes, pulling her to him as though they were tethered with invisible ropes.

He cocked his head and slowly inched his mouth closer to hers. The rapid beating of her heart filled her chest, making breathing difficult. She wanted him to kiss her.

EIGHT

Nicholas claimed her lips in a deep kiss. She fit perfectly in his arms. He didn't want to let her go. And yet he had to. He was protecting her. He needed to keep his emotions contained for both their own good.

Ending the kiss, he backed away. "Sorry. I shouldn't have done that. I have a job to do and that isn't part of it." If he said it enough, he might believe it.

She turned away, gathering up the dishes from the table. "I understand completely. Frankly, I don't have time. That's one of the reasons I keep things casual between me and anyone I've dated."

"So you're career focused?"

"Yes, aren't you?"

He nodded, but he didn't like her response. She loved children. She should be a mother. And that was another reason to keep his distance. He would never have children even if one day he married. His role model left a lot to be desired. All he knew was a cold, callous father who only warmed up around his wife, and a mother who only cared for her husband.

Selena brought the dishes to the sink, when chimes, like bells ringing, resonated in the silence between them. She washed off the plates while he strolled to the door, checked the peephole and then let in Senator Eagleton.

"Selena, you have a visitor."

"I'm not expecting…" Her voice faded as her gaze connected with her uncle's. "Have a seat, Uncle Preston," she said, gesturing toward the living room "I wasn't sure you knew where I lived. I haven't been here long."

The senator didn't move. "I can't stay long, but I wanted to make sure you were all right after what happened last night. I was assured you would get protection." The tall man glanced at Nicholas. "Are you it?"

"Part of it. Brooke Clark will be here at nights."

"Good. Someone isn't happy with you, Selena. Two attacks in less than one week." He looked right at Nicholas, saying, "I expect the best from you," then rotated toward the door.

"Wait. Why did you come all this way and only stay a minute?"

"I told you—to make sure you were all right."

"You could have called." Wonder sounded in her voice.

"I needed to see you with my own eyes. I know how tough you can be, and I wanted to make sure."

Selena swallowed hard. "Are you certain you can't stay for some coffee?"

Her uncle's expression softened. "No. I have a meeting in an hour, and I can't keep the vice president waiting."

She crossed the room. "Thanks for coming."

"I'll call you about having dinner or lunch away from the Washington scene."

"That'll be nice." Selena waited in the entrance until her uncle climbed into his town car.

Nicholas came up behind her and clasped her shoulders, feeling the tension beneath his fingers. He kneaded her muscles. "It looks like he's trying."

"I hope so. I don't want to close that door because when Erin returns, I want to have a family relationship with her, which also includes her father. She loves him."

"But you don't care about him?"

"I don't know. When I was young, I used to think of him as a father figure since I never knew my own. After a while, I realized what was really going on between him and my mother. I couldn't forgive him for disowning my mother, therefore me." She released a long breath. "I'm trying to do what the Lord wants us to do. Forgive and move on. I'm closer but not there completely. We don't have a big family. How could he turn his own sister away? His only niece?"

"Did your mom tell you why?"

"No."

"Why don't you ask him, then?"

Selena shut the door, threw the lock in place and then leaned back against it. "I just might do that, but I'm almost afraid to know."

"You? I thought you weren't afraid of anything."

"Everyone has fears. If they say otherwise, they're lying."

"What else are you afraid of?"

"The usual." She shoved off the door and headed toward the kitchen. "How about you?"

"Same answer—an evasive one."

"Okay, rats." She shuddered. "When I was a kid, I woke up with one on my chest staring at me. I haven't been able to shake that fear."

"Turning out like my father. My mother and making money were all he cared about."

"With the job you have, helping others is one of your priorities."

He chuckled. "True, but then I have my inheritance stashed away."

"I keep forgetting you were born with a silver spoon in your mouth."

"Good. It's not something I tell a lot of people."

"Then why me?"

"You're easy to talk to."

She tapped her chest. "Me?"

"It has to help you in your job. You work with a lot of people when you set up events."

"I didn't start out wanting to do that kind of work. I sort of fell into the job when I was an assistant for the president's chief of staff. When he went to the White House, he asked me to come along and work for him. When the job of White House tour director came up, the president asked me to take the job. He'd liked what he'd seen me do."

"My commanding officer knew General Meyer, and when I left the service, he recommended me for a position with the Capitol K-9 Unit. He knew how I felt about animals."

Selena began loading the dishwasher. "Would you change anything about what you did?"

"Not one minute. How about you?"

"No. I love a challenging job and mine is definitely that."

As they exchanged stories of their work, Nicholas realized just how easy Selena was to talk to. He'd shared more with her than most, especially in such a short time. It must be the close quarters while he guarded her.

On Sunday afternoon, Cassie Danvers greeted Selena and Nicholas in the foyer of the foster home, protected by a high fence, a security system and a guard with a dog. Selena thought of her own house and realized she had the same things except the high fence. All Our Kids foster home, which Harland Jeffries had founded on his property, was temporarily located in a safe house. On the night of the murder at the congressman's house, a child's mitten had been found near the crime scene and determined to belong to one of the foster children. None of the kids would admit to being out that night, though. The home, housemother Cassie Danvers and the children had all been targeted by the killer or accomplices, so All Our Kids had been relocated to this secret residence out in the country. Nicholas had received special permission from his captain to bring Selena along, but she'd had to wear a blindfold during the drive.

Cassie outstretched her arm toward Selena. "I'm glad you could come. Gavin told me you're the White House tour director and planned that fabulous Easter Egg Roll for the children."

Selena shook the hand of the petite woman who ran All Our Kids Foster Home. "Gavin?"

"He's our captain," Nicholas answered.

"And my fiancé." Cassie pointed into a great room. "They're waiting for Max. Oh, and you, too, Nicholas."

"Thanks, Cassie. I know who the real star is

in this team." Nicholas took Selena's hand, and they entered an area filled with all kinds of toys and children.

"The kids don't want for a thing. I think Gavin is spoiling them—and I know Harland Jeffries also often orders toys for Gavin to bring over—but who am I but the manager," Cassie said with a laugh.

First Brooke and now Cassie, happy and making plans to marry. Love was all around Selena. A secretary in the West Wing announced a few weeks ago she was getting married, too. That was good for some people—just not her.

A boy about six or seven jumped up and rushed toward them. "Max, you're finally here." He threw his arms around the rottweiler. "I've missed you."

More kids started crowding around.

"Tommy, let others greet Max, too," Cassie said to the child with sandy-brown hair and blue eyes.

The slightly built boy backed away, mumbling, "Sorry."

As the other children petted Max, Selena moved to Tommy, who stared at the floor. "Max is special, isn't he?"

The boy lifted his head and nodded. "I wish I could have a dog like him."

"I'm Selena, Tommy." She knelt down and

whispered, "I'll tell you a secret. So do I. Max is wonderful."

Tommy grinned, showing one of his missing teeth. "I just lost this." He pointed at his mouth. "I got a whole dollar for it. Cassie gave it to me." He dug into his jeans pocket and pulled it out. "All mine."

Selena's heart cracked, and all she wanted to do was hug the boy. She could remember, when she was growing up and got anything, how special it was, especially one Christmas when a charity gave out presents. She got a doll. She still had it.

"What are you going to do with the dollar?"

"Save it. I want my own bike, not one I have to share with the others."

After the children lavished attention on Max, Nicholas motioned them to the far side of the large room. "Are you all ready for a story?"

Several said yes, while others cheered.

Tommy hurried toward the group.

Cassie came up beside her. "I would never have pegged Nicholas as a storyteller, but he is. I think it surprised him when they all asked him to tell them a story after he'd read a book to them." She slanted a look at Selena. "I admit I'm surprised you received clearance to come here to the safe house."

There was a wealth of questions in Cassie's

voice, and her gaze assessed Selena. "He's been ordered to guard me."

The manager's eyes widened. "Why?"

"I've been attacked twice, and my home and office have been burglarized"

"I assume it involves the Jeffries case if the Capitol K-9 Unit is involved."

Selena nodded. "I'm Erin Eagleton's cousin. Like the Capitol K-9 Unit, maybe the attacker thinks I know where she is." Now that she'd said it aloud, she realized it was a real possibility. *Or the attacks were tied to the Littleton case or both.*

"Do you?" Cassie asked with a twinkle in her eyes.

Selena chuckled. "No, but if I did, I wouldn't be telling the captain's fiancée I did." She panned the group of children—their expressions were intense while listening to a story about the White House. "Have they ever been to the White House?"

"No."

"I'd love to give them a tour. I can make the arrangements."

"I'll take you up on that when the Jeffries case is settled and the murderer is in jail."

"Perfect." The loud clapping drew Selena's attention back to the children and Nicholas.

A few kids threw their arms around a grinning Nicholas. He would make a great father. Not one of the children hadn't responded to him.

"I'm glad we got away from the White House for lunch," Selena said a few days later as Nicholas pushed her chair into a white-clothed table at a popular restaurant nearby. "The West Wing has been busy this morning with meetings"

"I saw your uncle." Nicholas picked up the menu.

"I did, too. He even stopped and talked to me before he met with the president. Congressman Jeffries was there, too. Did you find out anything about who was peeking into his house?"

"Dead end. The shoe print was a woman's size, but only one camera caught her back. She was wearing a silk scarf, and besides, we know from the elderly couple who took her in before she disappeared again that Erin changed her hair color and style. Whoever it was made a point to disguise herself."

"But from the tone of your voice, you don't think the woman is Erin," she said as the waiter appeared at the table.

Nicholas waited until after they had ordered before replying, "No. I can't see why she would be at the congressman's house. I would think that would be one of the last places she would go."

"You've got a point."

"If I spot Erin, I'll let you know."

"And then you'd watch me like a hawk to see if she contacts me."

He pointed at himself, grinning. "Who, me?"

Out of the corner of her eye, Selena spied Carly Jones, Tabitha Miller and a couple of other aides to the senators and representatives at the White House. "It looks like we aren't the only ones escaping for lunch. Did you ever find out who was at Tabitha's that day Greg Littleton had an argument with Saul Rather?"

"Tabitha could only give me three names of who attended her get-togethers, Sally Young, Janice Neill and Becky Wright. Sally couldn't remember if she was there that day. But Becky Wright confirmed that Tabitha had shown some interest in Rather. That was why they were out on the balcony, since he was swimming. I think she was the one on the balcony with Tabitha."

"What about Janice Neill?"

"I haven't been able to track down Janice, who no longer lives in the area. It seemed those three were the regular attendees. I'm looking into how far Tabitha's interest in Saul Rather went. The problem is, the incident was almost two years ago."

The waiter delivered their iced tea, and Selena took a long drink. "I hope we can prove Greg didn't kill Saul. From my research into the case, I believe he's innocent."

"Perhaps Janice will have a better memory of what happened that day at the pool."

"So three regulars at these weekly get-togethers at Tabitha's with others occasionally dropping in."

Nicholas touched her hand, compelling her to look at him. "Don't sound so defeated. I know this is a long shot, but if Littleton didn't kill Rather, then we need to see who used the man as a scapegoat. I'm looking at the court records and police evidence with the mind-set Littleton is innocent."

As their lunch arrived, Selena watched Tabitha and Carly leave together after the other two aides. Outside in front of the large plate-glass window, the two women faced each other and, guessing from their expressions, the exchange wasn't a pleasant one. Did the animosity between Eagleton and Jeffries carry over to their staff?

While Selena enjoyed her spinach salad, she said, "I'd love to go back to the All Our Kids Home this weekend, but my uncle wants me to come to lunch on Sunday. I don't want you to cancel going to the home because you're protecting me. Could we go on Saturday instead?"

Reuben sandwich in his hands, Nicholas put it on his plate. "Yes, if you don't mind being blindfolded again?"

"Not one bit. Things have been calm the last

few days. Maybe the person who attacked me and trashed my house realizes I don't know anything."

"Don't count on that. You need to stay vigilant. We haven't been able to figure out who the person on the motorcycle was. There were no one else's fingerprints on the knife, and on the bike the only other prints belonged to the owner who, like Geary, had an airtight alibi. He was in a staff meeting with the press secretary."

"I especially want to see Tommy again. There's something about him that draws me."

"We've all tried to get Tommy to open up."

"About what?" She forked some salad and slipped it into her mouth.

"There's evidence one of the children from the foster home could have possibly witnessed Jeffries's murder. Tommy denies he is the one, but he's been having nightmares about a bad tall man with white hair."

"Harland Jeffries?"

"We talked about it, but his hair is gray, he was shot, too. The gun was never found at the scene of the crime. So where is it? Also a car was sighted speeding away from the house. Tommy's description of the man in his nightmare still leaves who it is inconclusive. Too vague. Lots of men have white hair, and it might not have anything to do with happened at Jeffries's estate."

Selena rubbed her chin and thought a moment. "Tommy would have had to sneak out at that hour to have witnessed the shootings. Most kids won't admit that."

"Cassie has stressed to the children no one will get into trouble if the one comes forward. Still nothing."

"But you think it's Tommy?"

"Yes. He has been upset a lot and withdrawn. Brooke worked hard to help him open up, but he's just too scared."

"Except around you and Max."

"That's because he loves dogs."

"A kid after your own heart."

His eyes crinkled with a big smile. "I used to go once a week when it was on Jeffries's property, but I didn't know Tommy well. I've been trying to get closer to the boy, and I have, but not enough for him to trust me."

"What if he really isn't the one?"

"Cassie is on the lookout for anything that indicates it could be someone else, and I'm getting to know all the kids even more than before."

Selena tapped her forefinger against her chin. "You know, this getting to know a person better in order to get information sounds like a familiar pattern of yours."

His tanned face deepened to a red shade. "You want to find out the truth as much as I do. And I really believe if Erin contacted you, you'd let me know."

Under his straightforward stare, she shifted in the chair, wondering if she would. And that question plagued her the whole way back to the White House. Would she turn in her cousin if given the opportunity? She didn't have an answer. She didn't trust many people. Could she trust Nicholas to look out for Erin's best interests?

At her office door, Nicholas's cell phone rang. He quickly answered it and frowned, turning away from her.

When he hung up and looked at her, she asked, "Was that about Erin? The case?"

"Yes, there has been another sighting—at the Capitol Building—of a woman in sunglasses and a silk scarf over her head who fits Erin's height and build. I'm meeting Isaac there to check it out. Remember, I'm your ride home."

"I'm not going to forget that." She watched him hurry away.

On Saturday at All Our Kids, Nicholas finished another one of his stories about a brave little boy who came forward and admitted he'd eaten all the candy. Then he told another one about a special zoo with unusual animals in it. Again Selena marveled that he could keep their attention, especially Tommy who sat near Max and petted him.

At the end, Nicholas looked at the children. "Now what I want from you are what do the animals in the zoo look like."

Selena and Cassie passed out paper, pencils and markers for the group to begin.

As the children started working, Cassie turned toward Selena and Nicholas. "I hope you'll stay for an early dinner."

"I'd love to," Selena said before Nicholas had a chance to voice his answer. She'd found a place she could donate some of her free time and wanted to get to know the children better.

For the next half hour, she and Nicholas walked around the room, helping different children with their pictures. At six, Cassie announced dinner and sent all the kids to wash their hands.

"It's not fancy. I hope you like macaroni and cheese." Cassie walked with Selena and Nicholas to the big dining room with two long tables. "Gavin was supposed to be here, but he was delayed and will be late."

As the kids filed into the room, the girls sitting at one table and the boys at the other, Cassie checked their hands before they sat.

Selena positioned herself at the boys' table and said to Nicholas, "I think we should mix things up. Don't break too many hearts this eve-ning." She winked at him and sank onto her seat.

Nicholas leaned down and whispered, "The same goes for you. I'm not sure how much I'll be able to contribute to the conversation if they talk about dolls, boys."

"I disagree. You should be able to give them great advice."

He headed to his place at the girls' table, and as he sat, they all giggled. He turned red and sent her a glare.

She ignored him, and after Cassie blessed the food, Selena scanned the boys on her right then on her left. At the other end of the table, a chair was empty.

"Is someone missing?" Then Selena real-ized there was, and it was Tommy. "Where's Tommy?"

The guys looked around, then the oldest near her shook his head. "He was with us in the bath-room."

"Could you go make sure he's all right?"

A tall, skinny boy jumped up and rushed from the room. He returned five minutes later and an-nounced to everyone, "Tommy is gone."

NINE

Everyone in the dining room went quiet.

Nicholas shot to his feet. "Thanks," he said to the boy who'd checked the bathroom. "You should eat your dinner before it gets cold. I'll check the house." He kept his voice calm while his thoughts raced with possibilities of where the seven-year-old could be.

The first place he headed was the security-system controls to see if it was on. Cassie had told him that when they were in for the night, she immediately turned the alarm on. If a child tried to go outside or someone attempted to break in, it would go off. When he inspected the box on the wall, he noticed it was still on.

Then Tommy should be in the house.

Selena came out of the dining room. "I'm helping you look. Cassie has gone to get her assistant, Virginia, from the kitchen. She'll stay with the children while Cassie starts with the downstairs."

"Good. Someone needs to be in the dining room to keep the kids calm. Although Cassie's assistant is a bit high-strung and might not be the best person for that, but we need all the help we can get. We'll search Tommy's room he shares with four other boys then work from there."

"Virginia seems so nice." Selena ascended the stairs with Nicholas.

"She is and great with the kids, but she worries a lot and can get dramatic."

In Tommy's bedroom, three sets of bunk beds were along the walls, four beds made while one was messy and another had only a bare mattress. As Selena inspected the top bunk and then under the bottom one, Nicholas opened the closet and inspected anyplace a boy would hide.

"Nicholas, the window is open."

He backed out of the closet and peered toward Selena, who had opened the curtains. She started to raise the window up the rest of the way, when he said, "Don't. If someone came in here and took Tommy, there may be prints."

Without touching anything, Selena studied the sill. "I don't think that's it. There's a sheet tied at the side." She held the drape totally back to show Nicholas one end was tied to a nearby bunk bed.

From the door with the curtains shut, it hadn't been obvious. Using a ruler he'd found on a desk, he painstakingly lifted the window without touching it with his fingers then leaned out. "There's only one sheet. He made it to the roof of the back porch." Nicholas pulled back and rotated toward Selena. "I'm going outside with Max. Continue to go from room to room, and if you or Cassie find Tommy, call me on my cell."

"Where's Max now?"

"In the great room. I was letting him rest." He started for the door. "I'm calling Gavin. We may need more team members with their dogs."

Nicholas left Serena to examine the rest of the rooms on the second floor. He made his way downstairs to Cassie, still in the dining room, and whispered to her what he was going to do and to have Gavin come as fast as he could with any of the team nearby.

Cassie turned a worried face up at him. "Anything else?"

"Check the rooms downstairs," he said as Virginia Johnson entered from the kitchen with a grim expression on her face.

The boy nearest Cassie chimed in, "We can help."

Nicholas scanned the children, some afraid, others concerned. "I'll find Tommy. The best thing you all can do is stay here and follow Cassie's and Virginia's directions."

"Tommy was upset when we went to wash our hands," David said.

Nicholas nodded. "Thank you for that information," he said to the child. "Cassie, can you get the jacket Tommy wore today when they played outside?"

She hurried from the dining room and returned a minute later. Her hand shook as she gave him the coat. She walked with him to the great room.

"I didn't want to say this, but I'm sending the guard inside after I talk with him. He'll lock the door and turn the alarm on as a precaution." He called Max and put the leash on him.

Pausing on the front porch, he waited until he heard the lock being clicked in place. He waved to the security guard with his dog and jogged toward him, Max trotting next to Nicholas. "I think Tommy sneaked out. I'm going to check the grounds, but I'd feel better if you were in the house until I figure out exactly what happened."

"How long ago?"

"No more than fifteen minutes ago."

"I've been on the front and left sides of the yard. I didn't see anything and Gus didn't indicate he was concerned about an intruder."

"He probably wouldn't since he's used to the kids. Tommy used the back porch. I'm not sure how he got down from there yet."

"I know. There's a trellis with climbing roses on it. If he's determined, he could have used that."

Remembering the knotted sheet, Nicholas headed for the vehicle. "He is."

"I don't see him getting over the fence with the barbwire on top, but he could hide in the woods at the rear of the property."

"Thanks." When Nicholas grabbed his flashlight from the Tahoe, then rounded the side of the house, he glanced at his watch. About another hour of light left. It was April, but the nights got chilly.

When he reached the back porch, he zeroed in on the trellis and found broken-off stems, and one thorn had blood on it. Fresh.

Nicholas let Max inhale the child's scent on the jacket then said, "Find."

Max sniffed the air and took off toward the woods, the area heavy with foliage. Nicholas could imagine a small boy crawling into the dense vegetation and hiding. But why? Did something scare him?

Max delved into the underbrush. Pausing every once in a while, his K-9 partner smelled the air then took off again. The forest became darker with a canopy of leafing trees above him.

Nicholas turned on his flashlight and yelled, "Tommy. Max is worried about you. Where are you?" Over and over he repeated the plea for the little boy to show himself.

Max stopped at a big bush, sat and barked.

"Tommy, are you in there?"

Silence.

"Everyone is worried about you."

A faint sound of sobs drifted to him. Nicholas knelt, parted some branches and shone the light into the dimness.

Tommy lifted his tear-stained face. "I can't go back." His words quavered as the green leaves did in the breeze.

"I thought you loved being here."

"Not anymore."

Nicholas's lungs seized his next breath and didn't release it for a full minute. "Did something happen today at the house?"

"I don't want anyone I care about being hurt. I'm not brave like the boy in your story." Tommy sniffled and knuckled his eyes.

"No one is going to get hurt. We won't let it happen."

"I'm fine. I'm staying right here, hiding." Tommy scooted back toward the oak tree the underbrush butted up against, determination evident in his crossed arms and his lower jaw jutted out.

"Okay." Nicholas twisted toward Max and said, "Stay." Then he crawled between the branches, fully loaded with leaves, and squeezed his body next to Tommy. "If you don't go, I won't, either. Here's your jacket in case you get cold." He held it out to the boy.

Tommy snatched the coat and quickly donned it, then went back to hugging his arms against himself.

"Is it okay if I call and let everyone know you're safe? Cassie is mighty worried. So are Selena, Virginia and all the kids."

"Kent doesn't."

"Your bunk mate?"

"Yeah. He makes fun of me crying. Says I'm a big baby."

"When did you cry?"

Tommy dropped his head, staring at the ground. "This morning."

"What made you cry?"

"The bad man."

"Did you have a nightmare?"

Tommy nodded his head several times.

"He's coming for me. I can't let him hurt anyone. I lost…" His bottom lip trembled, and he twisted away so Nicholas couldn't see his face.

"What did you lose?" he asked in a soft voice, wanting to hug the frightened child.

"Everyone I love."

"Who?" Nicholas touched his arm.

"Mommy. I don't have a daddy. I don't have nobody." He swiveled his head toward Nicholas, his eyes shiny. "Then Mr. Mike was killed. He was nice to me."

"How do you know Mr. Mike was killed?" He must be referring to Michael Jeffries.

"I saw…" His eyes grew wide. "Cassie told us." He lowered his head.

"Tommy." Nicholas waited until he had the boy's attention. "Did you sneak out of the home when Mr. Mike was killed?"

A long silence filled the air. An owl screeched nearby, and Tommy threw himself at Nicholas. The child clung to him. Slowly the boy's shaking body relaxed.

Nicholas hurt for Tommy. If he had witnessed the murder, the trauma would give anyone nightmares, especially a young child. "Tommy, I can help you, but you need to tell me. Did you sneak out of the house that night? It was cold. You would have needed a coat, hat—gloves."

The boy tightened his hold on Nicholas.

"Did you? You aren't in trouble. In fact, you can help the police find the bad man." He needed to call Selena and let her know he'd found the child, but he didn't want to stop Tommy from telling him what the team had been trying to get the boy to say since Michael's murder.

Tommy buried his face in the crook of Nicholas's arm.

"You know, Tommy, I lost my parents when I was a child. It was hard on me. They died in a small-plane crash in another country. I don't have much family, either."

The child stirred and pulled back in order to look at Nicholas. "You're alone, too?"

"God is always with me. He was when I was a child, too. When I was upset or sad, I turned to Him. When something troubles me, I give it to the Lord."

"I pray to Him every night." He drew away. "Are you sure He listens?"

"Yes."

"Then why am I still having nightmares?" Tears welled in Tommy's eyes.

"Maybe you're trying to remember something that's important. Talking about it can help. Have you sneaked out like tonight before?"

Tommy nodded, one tear released to slip down his cheek.

"Tell me about it." Nicholas held his breath, hoping the child would voice his fears.

"I wasn't stealing the gloves. I was only borrowing them."

"Whose?" The child's blue glove found near the crime scene at Harland Jeffries's house?

"David's. He was sick and couldn't use them. They were brand-new and my favorite color. Blue. I lost one. I'm having bad dreams 'cause I did." More tears ran down his face. "I'm bad."

"No, you aren't, Tommy. You were only borrowing them."

"I wasn't gonna be gone long."

"What did you do when you sneaked away? How did you lose the glove?"

"Bad. Bad." The child kept shaking his head.

What was he referring to? What he did? The man in his dreams? "No, you aren't."

"Bad man. He hurts people."

Was he talking about the man who had tried to get inside the original foster home on Jeffries's property? Or someone else? Michael Jeffries's murderer?

"What did he do, Tommy?"

"Nothing. I don't know." Fear gripped Tommy. He scrambled away until the tree trunk halted his progress again. He hugged his arms to him and began rocking. "I've got to get away."

"Come, Max." The rottweiler scooted under the bush until he wiggled his way to them.

"Max is here. You are okay." Nicholas spoke in a soft, soothing tone, giving Tommy time to calm down. "No one is going to let anything happen to you or the other kids. Nothing has at this home. You've been safe."

"Yeah."

"I'm calling to let everyone know I found you. Cassie and the others will want to know you're okay."

As though sensing the child was troubled, Max snuggled close to Tommy, who began petting him.

Nicholas called Selena's cell. When she answered, he said, "Tommy's fine and with me. We'll be back soon."

"Your captain and Isaac Black arrived a few

minutes ago. Isaac is outside with the guard. He was going to walk the perimeter of the fence. You might see him on the way back. Gavin will let him know about Tommy."

He lowered his voice. "Everything all right there?"

"No problems, except the kids are all concerned about Tommy."

"See you soon." Nicholas slipped his cell into his pocket. "Ready to go back? Your friends are going to be glad to see you."

"Kent isn't."

"He might be. They were worried. Ready to head back?" he repeated.

"Yeah. Can I lead Max?"

"Sure. He always loves playing with you."

Nicholas made his way out from the underbrush and waited while Max and Tommy crawled out. They started toward the house, Nicholas shining his flashlight to illuminate the path. Out of the woods, Nicholas glimpsed Isaac and his beagle, Abby, emerge from the trees near the fence line.

A few minutes later, the front door opened and Cassie scooped Tommy into her arms. "Don't do that again. You scared me. Promise me?"

"I won't."

Cassie plucked a leaf from Tommy's sandy-brown hair. "First, the children want to see you, then you can go into the kitchen and eat some dinner. Virginia saved you a plate. After that, a bath and bed."

Tommy moved inside, and the kids swarmed around him, all talking at once.

Cassie turned to Nicholas. "Thanks. I'm so glad you were here when it happened."

"So am I." He spotted Gavin, escorting Tommy toward the kitchen, the leash to Max still in the boy's hand. "He's scared the bad man from his dream will get him. Will hurt you all. He's upset that Kent is making fun of him crying when he wakes up from a nightmare. I don't know if that had anything to do with him leaving tonight or not. As you're aware, he's very fragile right now. He almost told me about the bad man. He did admit he sneaked out and lost one of David's gloves. He feels guilty about that."

"At least that's a step forward. I'll talk with him. Put his mind at ease about the bad man. I wonder if the man is the one who shot Michael and Harland or if he's the one Tommy remembers from the attack on the original foster home."

Nicholas frowned, remembering when that happened. "We can't let anyone know that Tommy was the boy who dropped the glove near the murder scene."

"I'll see what I can do to get more from him. Gavin will help, too."

"Where's Selena? We need to leave. I know it's getting close to bedtime for the kids."

"She's upstairs helping to get some of the young girls to bed first."

"I'll go fetch her." He rotated toward Isaac. "Thanks for coming out here in case we needed to put out a larger-scale search for Tommy."

"No problem. Lately it seems like I've been on a few wild-goose chases."

"Yeah, I heard about the Erin sighting."

"A dead end like the one at the Jeffries house. Gavin wants me to do a perimeter search even if Tommy was found, so Abby and I are getting back out there."

Nicholas ascended the stairs to the second floor, hearing a few giggles coming from the young girls' room. He paused in the doorway. Selena stood in the center of the room while the three girls' gazes were riveted on her. One child had her hand over her mouth, trying to contain her laughter.

Selena held up her hand, palm outward. "Honest. When I rose from that mud puddle—no, more like a muddy river—I was covered from head to toe. I even had to wipe it out of my eyes so I could see. That'll teach me to try following the big kids when they didn't want me to." She glanced over her shoulder. "I'm going to have to leave. Tommy is safe downstairs, and it's getting late. From what I understand, it's *way* past your bedtime."

As Selena went to each of the girls, she tucked them in then kissed them on the forehead and said, "Good night."

Nicholas could envision Selena as a mother. She'd told him she loved kids, and it was obvious when she was around them. Why wasn't she married, with children of her own?

He backed up as Selena came to the doorway and flipped off the overhead light. Two nightlights remained on, though. Then she stepped into the hall and closed the door shut.

A loud sigh escaped her lips. "I haven't done that in years. As a teenager, I used to help working mothers and often put their children to bed."

"You haven't lost your touch. Ready to leave?"

"Just as soon as I see Tommy with my own eyes. There are times I see him, and he's so sad. Breaks my heart."

"I know. Mine, too. But nothing can be done until this case is over." Especially for Tommy. He was a witness to something that happened at the congressman's house. What, he didn't know. But the child was in danger until everything was settled.

"He's probably still eating. Max is with him, so I need to get him."

At the bottom of the staircase, Selena angled

toward him. "The children had fun today. I'm glad this incident ended well."

The kindness and concern in Selena's expression touched Nicholas, reminding him again what a special lady she was. He lifted his hand and brushed a stray strand of hair from her forehead. Her blue eyes—the color of a calm sea—captured him and held him enraptured until he heard a cough. He looked over her shoulder and caught Gavin in the entrance to the dining room, a gleam in his eyes, Max next to his captain.

The moment of connection evaporated, and Nicholas wished he could bring it back.

"I figured you needed Max." Gavin bridged the space between them and gave Nicholas the leash. "I hope tomorrow is uneventful. We all need it."

"I set up a meeting with my uncle. Nicholas is going with me to my uncle's estate, so I don't know how uneventful it will be. I intend to ask him all about Saul Rather."

"I might need combat pay. See you Monday, Captain." Nicholas guided Selena toward the exit, wishing they could have one day off from the case.

The closer Nicholas came to the Eagleton estate in Maryland, the more shallow Selena's breathing became. The past few months, her uncle and she had been tap-dancing around each other. She wanted answers today about Saul Rather and also about her mother, and didn't intend to leave until she got them. If her uncle had something to hide concerning Saul, she needed him to come clean because every lead on the Littleton case was coming up empty.

"Are you okay?" Nicholas asked as he pulled up to the redbrick mansion with a small porch with white columns.

"Yes, or I will be when I get this over with."

"It's his loss if he doesn't swallow his pride and accept you into the family wholeheartedly."

She tried to smile but couldn't maintain it more than a second. "I know that here—" she tapped her temple then splayed her hand over her heart "—but not here. As a little girl I would dream of being saved by a knight in shining armor like in fairy tales. I used to think my uncle might, but after a while, I realized there was no such things as a knight coming to rescue a damsel in distress. I began to look at life realistically. Then I met Erin and we became good friends. Suddenly that dream of my uncle being in my life started haunting me." A constriction in her chest expanded, and she sucked in several deep breaths.

Nicholas ran his hand down her arm and captured her hand. Cold. Sweaty with her fear, this would be a death to her dream once and for all. "Remember, I'm here for you."

She moistened her dry lips and swallowed to coat her parched throat. "And I appreciate that. I need to do this. For years I denied I cared about my family. I need to put an end to my dream one way or another." This time she smiled into Nicholas's beautiful deep brown eyes. "Let's get this over with."

After retrieving Max from the back, Nicholas joined Selena on the walkway and started for the mansion, clasping her hand again as though to tell her she wasn't alone. She knew the reality. She'd always been alone.

A maid admitted them into the house, the foyer huge, elegant and opulent, reminding her of the family her mother had come from. "Senator Eagleton told me to show you to the gazebo. He has lunch set up there."

Selena, with Nicholas by her side, followed the young woman to a long veranda that overlooked a beautifully landscaped yard, full of flowers already blooming. She saw the gazebo at the end of a brick walk nestled in front of a stand of towering oaks and maples. "I know my way."

After the maid excused herself and returned to the house, Selena faced Nicholas. "I need to talk with him alone first. This conversation has been years in the making. I'll call your cell and you can join us. I won't say anything about Saul Rather until then."

"I understand. I'll stay here until you let me know otherwise."

Selena leaned over and petted Max, the feel of the animal comforting beneath her fingers. Then she descended the steps.

As she strolled toward the gazebo, she admired the different colors of tulips, other flowers she didn't know the names of and the cherry blossoms on a few trees scattered around the gardens. Tranquil. A place to commune with God's creation. Although unsure of the conversation she would have with her uncle, she began to relax with each step as if the Lord walked with her.

She mounted the steps to the gazebo. Her uncle stood, and as she came toward him, he moved forward, uncharacteristically clasped her by the arms and drew her to him.

The sound of a gunshot blasted the moment to shreds.

TEN

Nicholas paced the veranda, his attention switching between Selena and her surroundings. Her uncle hugged her. The sight gave Nicholas hope she would work everything out with the senator.

The crack of a gun going off hit Nicholas as though he had been shot. But the noise came in the direction of the gazebo and the stand of trees nearby. Two hundred yards away.

Clenching Max's leash, he flew down the stairs to the path, and instead of taking it, he raced through the immaculate flower beds—the most direct route to where Selena and the senator were. He scanned the area then returned his focus on the gazebo.

His heart beating a mad staccato, he pumped his legs harder while pulling his Glock from his holster. When he reached the gazebo, he prepared himself for the worst. One or both were dead.

Selena swiveled her head toward him, her eyes dilated. "It came from there." She pointed to the thick trees twenty feet away from them. "When Uncle Preston collapsed against me, I saw a black movement over there. I called 911. Go."

"I'll be back." Nicholas jumped over the shrubs on the perimeter of the small woods, Max's leash in one hand, gun in the other.

He spied evidence of trampled ground and a broken stem on a young plant. "Max, check it." When the rottweiler latched onto a scent, Nicholas said, "Find."

Giving Max a long leash, Nicholas jogged behind his K-9 zigzagging the diameter of the stand of trees. A motorcycle starting up reverberated through the woods. When Nicholas came out the other side, he caught sight of a bike zipping away on the road in front of the senator's estate, a person all in black seated on it. Max yanked on his leash, wanting to go after the assailant. He was too far away for Max to catch up with him, even if the K-9 managed to get over the six-foot-high chain-link fence.

"Stay."

Nicholas took out his cell phone and called the police and headquarters. By the time he talked to Isaac, he'd climbed the fence and reached the place where the bike must have been. "No license plate visible. An older Harley chrome and black. I informed the Maryland state police and they are coming. The senator was hit, but I don't know how serious. Selena is with him." He studied the ground nearby. "There are tire tracks and shoe prints. Looks like boots—small size—maybe nine."

"I'm coming. I want to get copies of the evidence, too. Who was the target?"

"I don't know. I'm going back to talk with Selena and, hopefully, the senator."

After he scaled the fence, he petted Max and gave him a treat. Nicholas made his way to the gazebo by way of the perimeter of the woods. He didn't want to disturb the evidence any more than he already had chasing the shooter.

When he returned to Selena, her uncle was alert, scowling, while she held a white handkerchief pressed into the upper left side of his back. Nicholas noticed there was no exit wound.

She glanced at him. "The ambulance is on the way. They should be here by now, but I don't hear any sirens."

The senator clutched her forearm. "This won't keep me down. I'll be fine in no time."

"Not until a doctor sees you and takes the bullet out of you."

If the bullet had gone through the senator, Selena would have been hit, too. The thought chilled Nicholas. Who was the target? Was this a second attempt on her life or was someone after the senator, too?

Selena paced the hospital room, checking every few minutes to see if her uncle had awakened yet. After his surgery earlier to repair the damage the bullet had done to his shoulder, he'd been brought to his room, where he would stay at least overnight, possibly a couple days. He told her again he would be fine and for her to contact his chief of staff about what happened, then he'd fallen asleep. Carly Jones was downstairs right now letting the gathering press know what had occurred at the Eagleton estate.

Finally exhausted from the stress and worry, Selena collapsed on a small couch and leaned her head back against the wall. She was safe. Her uncle was safe now. A police officer stood guard outside the door. She closed her eyes and tried to wipe her mind clear.

But the memories of earlier inundated her. Her uncle coming toward her, stepping in front of her and hugging her. And because he had, he'd been shot. *Instead of me.* The realization that *she* might have been the target iced the blood pounding through her veins. She shuddered and wrapped her arms across her chest.

She'd known it in the back of her mind and had refused to acknowledge the possibility until now. This had to do with her looking into the

Littleton case. It had all started then. She'd been investigating Michael Jeffries since Erin's disappearance and nothing had occurred until she'd gone to visit Greg in prison. Who had she made nervous enough to try to kill her? Had she discovered something and didn't know it yet? She needed to delve into the files she'd collected—at least the ones she still had. Some were gone, the files on her stolen personal tablet. She'd tried to rack her brains to reconstruct what she'd found, but with everything happening, she hadn't completely.

When the door opened, she straightened, tensing in spite of the fact her uncle was guarded. Everything was making her jumpy. She relaxed when she saw her uncle's chief of staff, a well-dressed woman with short brown hair and brown eyes.

Carly entered, glanced at her boss in bed and frowned. "The press can be brutal. They kept wanting to know if this had anything to do with the attempt on Harland Jeffries." She plopped into the chair near the couch.

"What did you tell them?"

"The truth. No one knows the motive behind the shooting, but the police are working on the case. The reporters want answers instantly."

"So do I." Selena breathed deeply, trying to calm her rapid heartbeat.

"Where's your handsome bodyguard?"

"Who?" Selena asked, knowing full well to whom Carly referred.

"Nicholas Cole. Who else? Do you have another gorgeous man following you around?"

"He's on his way. Should be here any moment." Then she hoped Carly would leave. She didn't care to socialize right now. With Nicholas she didn't feel the need to fill the silence with chitchat.

"The senator's shooting has caused quite a stir on Capitol Hill. I've been handling calls all afternoon and evening. I finally forwarded my calls to another aide. He'll let me know if there is anything critical I need to take care of." The woman relaxed in her chair, stretching her legs out as though she was settling in for the night.

"You don't have to stay. I'm his closest family member here. I'll call you if you're needed. I prefer he have quiet when he wakes up. No worries about work."

Carly's eyes grew round. "But—but…" She looked long and hard at Selena and didn't move to leave.

The door to the room opened, and Nicholas came inside.

Carly's gaze swept between Selena and him, then her uncle's chief of staff rose. "I'll leave you two alone." When she flounced toward the exit, she passed so close to Nicholas she nearly brushed up against him.

"What's wrong with her?" Nicholas asked when Carly was gone and took the chair she'd been in.

"I'm staking my territory. Since Erin isn't here, I'm stepping in as his nearest family member. I'm doing it for Erin—" her gaze shifted to her uncle "—and for him. If it hadn't been for him, I would have been shot."

"Do you think he saw something and did that to save you?"

"I don't know, but I'd like for a little while to think my uncle loved me enough to try to save me."

"I know he can be a hard, demanding man, but when we had lunch last week, I didn't get that sense from him. In fact, I think he was acting a bit awkward, as if he didn't know what to do with you."

Love me. Accept me. Those words slipped into her thoughts unexpectedly and caught her off guard. She'd always thought of herself as tough, a loner who needed no one.

"Selena?"

She focused on Nicholas only feet from her, a man who had been there for the past couple of weeks, and realized she cared for him—beyond a friend. Maybe she was just vulnerable right now, with what was going on.

She cleared her throat and swallowed hard.

"Sorry, thinking about today. Did you get any leads from the crime scene?"

"Tire tracks from the motorcycle. I think the bike was picked up at an intersection on that road close to I-95. The police are looking for it, but I wouldn't be surprised if it was stolen, like the one in the underground parking garage. The person was dressed all in black like the other one."

"The same attacker?"

"It makes sense, but how did he know the senator was in the gazebo, and if you were the target, that you'd be there at that time."

"Followed us?"

"I didn't see any motorcycle or someone following us and, believe me, I checked a lot on the trip to your uncle's." His forehead creased. "No, I think the shooter was waiting."

"Which probably means I was the target, or he would have shot the senator earlier."

"Although we need to consider both options, that's my thoughts, too. It had to be someone who knew you were meeting with your uncle."

"I've been thinking. These assaults are tied to the Littleton case."

"You're probably right." One corner of his mouth tilted in a half grin. "I'm not going to let him have another chance. I'm pulling Isaac's help in on the Littleton case. We need to find that aide who was at Tabitha's the day Littleton had the argument with Rather at the pool. Janice Neill might remember who was there that day since the others didn't."

"We can't count out them, but maybe Janice will be able to help. Have you found out anything about Tabitha and Saul?"

"They went out but weren't dating at that time. The few people I talked to said there was no indication it ended on a bad note."

"I wonder who ended it."

"According to two busybodies at the apartment complex, Tabitha, so what would be her motive for murdering Saul?"

"Okay, if she wasn't rejected, maybe Saul was harassing her. From what I hear about her, she isn't a wimp and wouldn't take much from anyone."

"Don't you think she would have told her friends at the time?" Nicholas asked. "Sally, Janice or Becky?"

"Probably. I don't see her being quiet about it."

"I'm still looking into her, especially her whereabouts when certain incidents went down."

"Does she have an alibi for the time I was run down in the garage? The person riding the bike could have been a female. It happened so fast I'm not sure about much other than the attacker was dressed all in black with a dark motorcycle helmet."

"No alibi. Claims she was home alone, and I will be asking her about today, too. What I saw was from a distance as the shooter went over the fence. The person was a smaller man or a bigger woman."

"That fits Tabitha. I know there's no love lost between my uncle and Harland. What if she was dating Saul to get information about Uncle Preston's activities? Someone hired the PI to report on the visitors to Littleton. Lots of questions, no answers."

"Maybe Tabitha was using Saul. She wouldn't be the first here in Washington." Nicholas sat forward and grasped her hands. "How are you holding up?"

"I'm okay."

One of his eyebrows lifted. "Are you?"

"I'm not one of those women who fall apart at the sight of blood."

"Men do, too."

She sent him a small smile. "What I'm trying to say is I'll be okay with time. It was traumatic, but sadly not my first time to hold a person who had been shot."

"When?"

"A good friend in high school angered a gang member in the neighborhood and was wounded in a drive-by shooting." Talking about that sunny day when she'd turned sixteen brought back a rush of memories. The fear of her friend dying. Jasmine clinging to her until the paramedics arrived. The blood that covered Selena and trying to scrub it off her and feeling as if she hadn't succeeded.

Nicholas gave a low whistle. "Did your friend live?"

"Jasmine did, but she basically lost the use of her left arm." The tears she'd refused to shed when it happened surged to the foreground. She swallowed over and over, but they still wanted their release after all these years.

"Did the gang member go to prison?" Nicholas moved to the couch and sat beside her.

"No, he was killed in a shootout." The words came out in a hoarse stream as tears ran down her cheeks.

Nicholas slipped his arm around her and pulled her against him. He held her while she cried, wetting his shirt. His quiet support reinforced her growing feelings for him, but everything was such a mess. She felt as though she were on a merry-go-round that would never stop and was picking up speed, the world flying by.

"My childhood was very different from yours, but I've had my share of caring for a wounded buddy while waiting for medical help to come or in some cases until he died. War isn't for the faint of heart, and it sounds like you lived in a war zone while growing up."

"My home wasn't in the thick of things, but some of my friends lived in the middle of it. I'd been visiting Jasmine that day."

"I'm—sorry," her uncle murmured in a raspy voice.

Selena pulled from Nicholas's embrace and twisted toward the bed. Uncle Preston's eyes, half-open, were fixed on her. She rose and went to him. "How are you doing?"

"I've had—better days. Water. Please."

Selena poured some into a plastic cup and helped him drink. When he finished, he relaxed back on the pillow, his eyes closing.

Nicholas approached her. "Why don't I go get you something to eat and bring it back here, unless you want to go with me to the cafeteria downstairs."

"No, I need to stay in case he wakes up again. I want him to see a friendly face." *And find out why he said, "I'm sorry."*

While Nicholas was gone, Selena sat in the chair close to the bed. She wanted to be right there when her uncle awakened again. How much had he overheard of the conversation with Nicholas about Jasmine?

Not long after that incident, she'd paid her uncle a visit because her mother had insisted Selena be the one to ask him for financial help.

She'd watched Uncle Preston and Erin from a distance but never approached them. She couldn't bring herself to do it. He'd rejected her mother's attempts, and Selena couldn't take it if he rejected her. That was the day she'd resolved she would rise above her circumstances and prove to the world—to her uncle—she was a worthy person. She didn't realize until later that in the Lord's eyes she was worthy no matter her circumstances. Once she'd figured that out, her fight to prove herself changed. She'd wanted to make a difference in people's lives. As the White House Tour Director and assistant to the president, she'd found a way to influence policies that benefited the huge number of people and groups who wanted to visit the White House and also plan special events like the Easter Egg Roll for children.

Her uncle stirred, but his eyes remained closed. Selena reached out and touched his hand. He could have died today without knowing Erin's fate. She was going to do all she could to get Erin back safely and cleared of any suspicions concerning Michael Jeffries's murder.

"I'm going to make sure Erin comes home soon," Selena whispered, coating her dry throat.

Her uncle squeezed her finger and rasped, "We both will."

"Do you want some more water?"

"Please." His eyes slowly opened and latched onto hers.

She felt his stare as she poured some liquid into the cup then brought it to his mouth, holding him up to drink. When he indicated that he had had enough, she put the water on the bedside table then turned toward him. "Anything else?"

He nodded slightly, swallowing hard. "Your forgiveness."

Her heartbeat slowed. She never thought she would hear her uncle say that to her. Maybe he didn't know what he really was doing. "For what?"

"For letting my relationship with my sister…" His eyes slipped closed.

No! Please finish what you're saying.

Her uncle looked at her again. "Affect ours."

She wanted to understand why he had. What did her mother do to make him turn away from her? She pressed her lips together. This wasn't the time to talk about it, but she would later.

"Did they catch…who shot me?"

"No, not yet, but they're following several leads. Did you see anything?"

Silence dominated for a long moment, then he took a deep breath and let it go slowly. "Not much. A flash of black. It happened fast. I tried…" Again he shut his eyes.

"What?"

"To protect you."

Emotions clogged her throat, and she tried to fill her lungs with oxygen-rich air. "Thank you," she said in a hoarse whisper. *I don't care about the past. I forgive you.* But she kept those words inside, not quite ready to openly admit her need for a family.

"I wasn't going to let you get hurt…again."

She smiled and took his hand between hers. "Do you know who knew you would be in the gazebo or that I was visiting?"

"If I'm at my estate, I usually eat my lunch at the gazebo on Sunday."

"It's gorgeous, as are your gardens. Who knew about me?"

"My staff." He frowned, his eyes drifting closed. "I think…that's all."

She waited to see if he'd say anything else, but he didn't. He'd fallen asleep again. Selena slipped her hands from his and rose, stretching. Then she began pacing once more, pausing at the window to look out at the darkness descending. Where was Nicholas?

Before coming to the hospital, Nicholas had taken Max to Selena's house. He was glad he had because he would stay with Selena tonight in the senator's hospital room. He didn't want her alone that long, even with a guard on the door. He couldn't shake the sensation that she had been the target today. Before heading into the cafeteria, he stepped outside, where cell reception was better, to call Isaac to see if he'd discovered any clues to who was behind the shooting.

"Anything new?" Nicholas asked Isaac when he answered, inhaling the welcomed fresh air without the scent of the hospital infused in it.

"The motorcycle was found, stolen like the other one and left abandoned."

"We need to check and see if anyone involved in the case has ridden a bike. This attacker wasn't a beginner, not from what I saw the night of the garage assault or today."

"I'll have Fiona run a check in the morning. I just came from talking with Tabitha Miller. She doesn't have an alibi. She says she went for a drive. I had to wait until she showed up."

"When?"

"An hour ago."

"Did she say where she'd been? That she'd stopped for gas, something we can check?"

"She said she drove to Solomons Island where she walked along the pier. She didn't stop for gas or to eat. I'll do some checking on traffic cams and see if I can verify her whereabouts, at least her car's whereabouts."

"I'm surprised she didn't eat or stop somewhere." In the distance Nicholas saw someone who looked like Erin with a black wig on walking toward the hospital entrance. He took a few steps in that direction.

"That's what I thought. I can't rule her out yet."

The woman stopped, stared at him then whirled about and ran toward the parking lot. "I've got to go." Nicholas pocketed his cell and gave chase. If it was Erin and he could catch her, a lot of questions could be answered.

ELEVEN

Selena checked her watch for the tenth time in half an hour. What if something had happened to Nicholas? He should have been back by now, even if the cafeteria was crowded.

The sound of the door swishing open made her tense at the same time that relief flowed through her. She pivoted toward the entrance. The sight of Nicholas with a tray full of food made her sag and ease down on the sofa, her legs trembling.

"It's about time. I was thinking all kinds of things happened to you."

"Sorry, but I thought I saw Erin and chased her." He set the tray on a table and pulled a black wig from his back pocket. "I didn't catch whoever wore this, but if you can get a shirt from Erin's place, I'll run a test with Max tomorrow. My plan is to let Max sniff one of Erin's shirts, then I'll hide the wig and command him to find it. If the scent of Erin's shirt leads him to the wig, it was Erin at the hospital earlier."

"If it was her, at least I'll know she is alive."

"We'll see if your uncle will help us tomorrow, unless you have a key to her home. I'm having Isaac pick the wig up and see if Forensics can pull hair with DNA from inside it."

"I don't have a key to Erin's place, but I'm sure my uncle will give you access." Selena removed the covers over the food and drew in a deep breath. "I'm so hungry. I could eat cardboard right now."

"Save some for me. I'll be right back."

"Where are you going now?"

"To get an evidence bag from my car for the wig."

Selena was halfway through a club sandwich when Nicholas returned with the bag. "If you don't hurry, I might eat your food, too."

He put the bag with the wig inside on a vacant chair and settled next to her on the couch. "The woman I chased earlier got away in a cab, but I couldn't see its number. Isaac is running down taxi pickups in the area. Maybe we'll be able to find out where she was dropped off."

"Don't sound so excited. If it was Erin, she's innocent."

"She needs to come in and tell her side of the story. It might help us make sense of what's been happening. If she was the one out in the parking lot, that means she heard about her father being shot. General Meyer made sure it hit the news big-time that it was touch and go with the senator."

"So you were hoping Erin would try to see her father?"

"Yes."

"Why didn't you tell me?"

He dropped his gaze.

"Nicholas?"

"I didn't want you to worry. The guard at the door knew, and a plant on the floor was here keeping an eye out for her. Also hospital security and another guy in the lobby."

"If I didn't know better, I would think you planned my uncle's shooting."

He glared at her. "I'll forget you said that. You do know me better than that."

"Yes, but think about what Erin is going through right now. Not knowing how her father is doing."

"We'll update the press first thing tomorrow morning. I'm sure she won't come back after seeing me."

"How does she know you?"

"Remember, my grandfather was a senator and an acquaintance of your uncle's. I saw Erin at several events and we spoke a couple of times. She knows I work for the Capitol K-9 Unit."

"Do you believe my cousin is innocent of

Michael's murder?" Steel ran through her voice because she'd thought he'd gotten past the idea that Erin was guilty.

Nicholas twisted toward her. "Why is she running? Why doesn't she come forward and explain what happened?"

"Because the real killer is after her."

"Then we can protect her. She should know that."

The food in her stomach solidified. She rose and towered over him, anger churning in her gut. "I think you should leave before I say something I'll regret."

"I'm *not* leaving. I'm guarding you." When she continued to glare at him, he said, "I didn't say she was guilty. I think she's in trouble. If she didn't kill Michael and shoot Harland Jeffries, then I agree she's running from who did. She most likely has information we need to solve the two crimes. That's why I want her to come in. She may need to be protected, too."

The appeal in his eyes tore down her defenses. She sank onto the couch next to him. "That makes sense. Then why are you helping me with the Littleton case if you don't think she murdered Michael?"

"Because you riled someone when you starting delving into the case. Did Michael, too, and that's what got him killed? Even if that isn't the motive for Michael's murder, I want justice served for Littleton—if he's innocent—and to find out who really did murder Rather. But even more than that, you're in danger. If something happened to you, I wouldn't be able to forgive myself for turning away from you when you needed me."

His declaration soothed any remnants of her earlier anger. "Then we're going to continue looking into the Littleton case?"

"Yes. We know the person has access to the White House and knew that you were going to be at your uncle's today. Also, someone on Eagleton's staff hired the PI to keep tabs on Littleton's visitors."

"That's still a long list. People in this town talk. It wasn't a secret we were meeting. I think I mentioned it to several at the White House."

"Who?"

"For one, Ann, General Meyer's secretary. One of the president's secretaries and the nurse who was on duty the day of the Easter Egg Roll. So from there, no telling who heard. We were talking about our plans for the weekend."

"In other words, anyone possibly in the White House or who visited recently."

"Yes. I never considered someone was outright trying to kill me. I thought the incident in the garage was solely for grabbing my tablet for information like the one I had at my house. I was excited my lunch with my uncle might lead to a reconciliation. Ann and I are good friends, and I was telling her, when others joined us. For that matter, I'm sure General Meyer knew."

"So since the whole world knows, it's futile to match the list of people at the White House when you were attacked in the parking garage with the ones who knew about the lunch date?" Sarcasm laced his words.

"No, go for it. It will probably take a few people off the list."

His eyes gleaming, he chuckled. "You still have some of your sandwich to finish. I don't want you to say I didn't feed you while I was guarding you."

With her appetite back, Selena finished her meal, comforted by the fact Nicholas sat next to her. He obviously thought that the shooter had intended to kill her, not the senator, confirming her own suspicions, which meant Erin could soon be able to come home—if Selena could stay alive long enough to find Saul Rather's real killer. That person could be the murderer of Michael, too.

The next afternoon Selena entered her uncle's hospital room after returning from the White House with some work she had to attend to. She wanted to be near if Uncle Preston needed her, and his chief of staff as well as General Meyer had insisted on it, especially when they weren't sure who the assailant was and if the person was attached to the White House.

"Where's your young man?" her uncle asked, sitting up in bed, alert and ready to go home.

"He brought me up here and is leaving to get his dog at headquarters and to check in with his captain on any developments in the shooting yesterday. Has your doctor been in yet to release you?"

"Not soon enough for me. Probably in the next hour. Sit. I have something to talk to you about."

His serious expression set off alarms for Selena. She made her way to the chair by the bed and eased down onto it. "What's wrong?"

"You ask that question when someone tried to kill one of us yesterday? I'm worried about your safety."

She hadn't expected him to say that. The fact he was concerned encouraged her that their relationship would develop over time. "I'm worried about yours, too. You've been hurt. The doctor said another inch over, and you would have been seriously wounded."

He waved his hand in the air as if that didn't mean anything to him. "I want you to stay with me at my house. My town house in Washington, DC, has exceptional security, better than my estate. Carly had a consultant looking at it this morning to beef up anything needed to make it top-notch. I'll be staying there until my home in the country is as secured."

"I appreciate the offer, but my home is fine, especially with Nicholas or Brooke there." There was a part of her that wanted to jump at the chance to get to know him better immediately, but her cautious side caused her to hesitate. Any true change in their relationship had to come naturally if it was going to last.

"I won't be able to rest like I should if I'm constantly worried about your well-being. With Erin's disappearance, that's all I've been doing. Don't make me have to with you, too. Please." That last word almost seemed torn from him.

Selena clamped her lips together to keep from grinning. He probably wouldn't appreciate it.

"Besides, I want your Nicholas to find my daughter. I know she's alive." He laid his hand on his chest. "I know it in here. I heard you and him talking last night."

"You eavesdropped on our conversation?"

Her uncle smiled. "Not exactly. It was my room, and you two were sitting there talking."

"You could have let us know."

"In my defense, I was going in and out of consciousness, but I heard enough to know you believe the Littleton case could prove Erin is innocent of killing Michael and shooting Harland. I'll help you two any way I can. All day I've been thinking about those months Saul Rather was an intern on my staff."

"Did you remember anything that might help us?"

"At the young age of twenty-three, he was a Casanova. I may be busy, but I try to keep up with what my staff is doing."

"One person we know he dated was Tabitha Miller, an aide for Congressman Harland. Anyone on your staff?"

"I frowned upon that, but it didn't stop him from flirting with all the ladies."

"With Erin."

"He tried, but she wasn't interested. So you see, you'll have unlimited access to me if you stay at my DC house." His grin grew.

"Okay. Fine. Nicholas will be coming, too. He's been guarding me." And something told her he wouldn't turn it over to her uncle and his staff.

"It will be interesting to see how he's changed since he was a boy."

She wondered if this was the time to approach him about her mother, but as she was thinking about how to phrase the question, the doctor came into the room.

"Good. It's about time. I was ready to go home hours ago."

As her uncle and his doctor talked, Selena wrestled with even saying anything to Uncle Preston. Should she accept that he was changing his attitude toward her and not delve into why he'd turned away from his only sibling? What if she didn't like what he told her? She was trying to forgive her uncle for his coolness toward her. She didn't want anything to ruin that. Their relationship was so fragile she didn't know if it could weather his reasons.

Nicholas paused at the entrance into the den at Senator Eagleton's town house and enjoyed watching Selena working on a laptop concerning plans for a big event at the White House in celebration of the Fourth of July. He'd noticed when she was thinking seriously she often twirled her hair. At the moment it was entwined around her finger, and her facial features were set in concentration, her forehead knitted.

Suddenly she glanced up from her computer screen and looked right at him. "How long have you been there?"

"A couple of minutes. I was debating whether to bother you or not. Then you took the decision out of my hands." He moved into the room and settled near her on the couch. "I've got Max fixed up in the kitchen. He's met the guards at the back and front doors. I wanted him to be able to roam freely through the whole house."

"When this is over with, he's going to need a vacation."

"I totally agree. I'm going to take him camping in the Blue Ridge Mountains for a long weekend. Have you ever gone camping?"

"Me, camping? My idea of roughing it is a two-star hotel."

He studied her then burst out laughing when he saw the mischief in her eyes. "Not you. I know the area where you grew up. Camping would be a step up."

"On a more serious note, I don't like camping because you're vulnerable to all kinds of creatures, especially bears."

"That's why Max goes with me. He's a great warning system."

"That's what I love about Max. I feel safe with you and him here. I have a lot to do between now and the holiday, and it helps to be able to fully concentrate on what I need to accomplish."

"I hope you aren't going to open the White House to the public as you did for the Easter Egg Roll."

"Not the building, but the grounds will be used extensively. Besides, you can't see fireworks very well inside."

"You've got a point there." He wondered if the case would be solved by then. He hoped so. Erin was important to Selena, and he was discovering what was important to Selena was to him, too.

"Did your uncle talk about this Saturday night?"

"No, when he came home yesterday, he went

to bed. Since he woke up this morning, he hasn't rested with the parade of folks coming to see if he's all right. It wore him, out and I finally persuaded him to rest."

"On Saturday, even more people will be coming to see him. Before Carly left earlier, she told me about this fund-raiser your uncle is hosting at his estate Saturday evening. He insisted on going forward and forbade Carly from canceling the party. She thought it might be too much for him."

Selena shut her laptop and set it on the coffee table in front of her. "And she's right. I'll say something to him. Maybe he can postpone it a couple of weeks. He isn't up for reelection anytime soon. Who's he raising money for?"

"One of his favorite charities, supporting our returning veterans and their families. Eagleton Foundation gives a lot to the charity. It's a good cause."

"So you want him to have it only days after being released from the hospital?"

Nicholas held up both of his hands. "I didn't say that. But if he does have the party, he doesn't have to be there the whole time. I know the guy that heads Wounded Heroes. He can manage without your uncle there."

"What about the security at the party?"

"If he doesn't postpone it, I'll work with your

uncle and Carly on that. You aren't to worry about it."

Selena started to pick up her laptop.

Nicholas stopped her and drew her toward him. "No more work today. You hardly got any sleep the past couple of days."

"That couch in my uncle's hospital room wasn't comfortable. But it was better than the chair you were sleeping in."

"Sleeping? That's a stretch for what I was doing. More like resting my eyes. Too much noise for me to sleep. You know, hospitals aren't that quiet in the middle of the night."

"That's why my uncle insisted on coming home right away. He said he'd get more rest here than at the hospital."

Nicholas wrapped his arms around her and tugged her against his chest. "How about you? You need to take care of yourself."

She tilted her head back and looked at him. "I have you to do that. Isn't that part of being my protector?"

The teasing note in her voice captivated him. He loved seeing this fun side of her. He leaned her back against the arm of the couch, his mouth hovering above hers. Caressing her hair, he couldn't resist anymore the strong urge to kiss her. His lips touched hers. All his feelings toward her swelled to the surface.

He pulled back a few inches, their breaths mingling. "When this is over, we need to talk."

Her dreamy expression slowly faded. "When what is over?"

"Me having to protect you. The last thing I should do is kiss you." His words sobered him, and he straightened.

She sighed. "You're right. I'm never going to get my work caught up with you hanging around."

She infused humor into her voice, but deep in her eyes, he glimpsed concern. Selena wasn't used to depending on anyone else. From what she'd said about her past, it had become a necessity to do everything herself in order to accomplish all she had. He understood that. In many ways, he'd raised himself as Selena had done, just under vastly different circumstances.

He noticed her looking at her laptop sitting on the coffee table. "Is that your way of telling me to get lost?"

"Not too far. You are my protector, at least in General Meyer's and the president's eyes."

"How about yours?"

"I'm not sure. You confuse me."

He'd expected her to say yes or no. "How?"

"We're different in so many ways but the same, too. We should have nothing in common, but I'm discovering we do have a lot. We're both workaholics and enjoy our jobs. We grew up alone although there were many people around us. We both love Max." A smile brightened her eyes. "What's not to love about Max?"

"You're straightforward and so am I. And you like coffee the way I do—black and strong. And I believe we've shared things with each other we don't usually tell others."

"Your faith is strong. I saw that when we went to my church. When I thought I might have lost Erin, I began to question God. I'd wanted a relationship with my family, and Erin and I were becoming close like sisters. Then she vanished. I fought so hard my whole life and that hit me hard. Now I see I need to give it to the Lord. The only thing I can control are my actions and attitude. I can't control what's happening with Erin. It's ultimately in His hands. I need to trust Him."

Nicholas cupped his hand over hers. "Trust is hard to give to another, even the Lord, especially for people like us. But you're right. Ever since I left home, I've been running from my past. I turned my back on my family and although my parents are dead, I have neglected what they left behind. I haven't been home since I left years ago. I have caretakers watching over the estate, but it could be in ruins and I wouldn't know."

"You said once you grew up in Maryland. Is it near my uncle's place?"

"About thirty minutes away."

"Then I hope you'll take me to it one day. I want to see where you grew up."

"Only if you will show me where you lived." He didn't know if he'd want anyone to go with him and he was pretty sure Selena wouldn't want him going with her.

She opened her mouth but closed it and averted her gaze for a long moment. Then she turned and said, "A deal."

"Really?"

"Yes. I think where we grew up will always be part of us. Like you, I haven't gone back to the neighborhood since I left. Of course, I'm sure the landlord didn't take care of where I lived like the caretaker did with your estate." One corner of her mouth tilted.

Suddenly their conversation took on a lighter tone, and he was thankful for that. Selena had a way of getting him to say and do things he usually held back. "Did you talk to your uncle about getting an article of clothing from Erin's house?"

"Yes, and in fact, he gave me the key. I forgot about it when I started working." Selena dug into her jeans pocket and pulled it out. "When are we going? I'm anxious to know if it was Erin at the hospital. Uncle Preston is, too."

"We're not going. I'm sending Brooke tomorrow morning. We'll know something shortly after that. She'll bring the wig, which the forensics lab ran their tests on today. They found hair, the color we were told Erin had dyed hers, but DNA couldn't be pulled from the strands. So no confirmation that way."

"I know in my heart it was her. I can't answer for the other sightings. Erin would be drawn to the hospital to see about her dad."

"Maybe the senator was the target, after all. What if someone was trying to lure Erin out of hiding?"

"The real person who killed Michael and wounded the congressman? Hmm. That makes sense. So does that mean you don't have to follow me around?"

He chuckled. "Nope. We don't know for sure who the shooter was targeting, but we do know you were assaulted in the underground garage. You're stuck with me."

"I guess it could be worse," she said with a laugh. "Now go so I can work another hour or so until dinner." She shooed him away.

"I guess that's my cue to walk Max around the yard. He needs to go outside."

At the entrance into the room, he sent her a woebegone look that only made her laugh more.

The next morning, in the glassed-in back porch, Selena stood at the floor-to-ceiling window and stared out at the gorgeous day. This was as far as she would go to enjoy it. Since the glass was bulletproof and several guards patrolled the grounds, Nicholas had agreed she could work here and enjoy the blooming flowers from a distance. She wanted her life back, but that wasn't going to happen until Nicholas discovered who had come after her.

"I see you've found my secret retreat. This is one of my favorite places at my town house, even in the winter."

Selena rotated toward her uncle standing in the doorway, his arm in a sling. Some color had returned to his face since the shooting. "How are you doing today? You slept in."

"Better. By the time of the party this weekend, I'll be back to my old self." He glanced down at his bandaged arm. "Except for this. My doctor wants me to use the sling for the rest of the week, but I'm ditching it for the party."

"Are you sure?"

"I don't want people to see me as a victim."

She knew that feeling. She hadn't, either. That was why she'd worked her way through college. "I know you don't have to run for the Senate anytime soon, but your sling could give you the sympathy vote."

He frowned. "No, the only way I want people's votes is the straightforward way, that my stand and platform are similar to what they want. In my youth, I made some bad decisions because of how something would appear to my constituents. Image was important. When Erin was splashed all over the news, I didn't care about what the voters thought. All I wanted was my daughter back safe, but we still don't know if she is alive. That is my reality check." Her uncle slowly moved toward her. "I think we need to talk."

"Yes." She waited until he took a seat on a white wicker love seat with green cushions, then she sat in the nearby matching chair. She resisted the urge to place her hand over her heart as if that would stop it from beating rapidly. "What do you want to talk about? The Littleton case?"

"No, but I want you to know that I had Carly check into my staff members to see if someone in the office hired that private investigator, Mr. Goodwin, to track the comings and goings of anyone who visited Littleton in prison. So far, she can't find anything. No money was used from my funds."

"It could be someone not in your office. The private investigator never met the person."

"That's what I think, but that's not what I want to talk about. The case is in good hands with Nicholas and you. I owe you an explanation of why I disowned your mother."

She didn't know if she wanted it now. They had taken steps to build a relationship. She didn't want anything to destroy that. "You don't—"

"Yes, I do," he interrupted, his mouth twisting into a hard line. "I don't know what your mother told you, but I didn't totally kick her out. She left with part of her inheritance from our parents that wasn't tied up."

"She did?" All she could remember her mother talking about was how she'd left with only the clothes on her back.

"Yes, and she blew through the sizable amount in three years. That's when I denied her access to the rest because I was the executor of my parents' will. There were stipulations she had to meet before she would get any more of it. One was she would stop drinking and would go into rehab. On the surface she pretended she was trying, but within a week had left. She finally refused and started openly taking drugs with the alcohol."

For a second, Selena closed her eyes, hating to see the pain in his expression mixed with disgust. She'd fought that for years—feeling sorry for her mother, then so upset she couldn't stand to be around her.

"The last straw was when she made a spectacle of herself at a huge game-changing fundraiser for my first campaign for a congressional seat. I lost a lot of my funding and support. The following month I lost the race by a narrow margin." He locked gazes with her. "I reacted with anger and told her I never wanted to see her again. That was the last time I did. I was—still am—stubborn."

"What did she do?" She remembered how many times her mother had embarrassed her and she'd been so mad that she finally ran away at seventeen. Although she had seen her mom some in the years afterward, she had never forgiven her for her actions.

"She got drunk at a function with investors and started a brawl that escalated and the police were called. The photo of her handcuffed, looking drunk, was all over the news for several days. Then she turned right around and shoplifted, again for attention because she had the money to pay for the clothes she took. She was sick, but I didn't know what to do for her anymore. She refused any help from me and wouldn't see a therapist."

Selena dropped her gaze to a spot on the floor between them. "She didn't want to stop. I think all she lived for was her next drink or fix. I couldn't watch her destroy herself, so I can understand how you felt."

"I knew we couldn't have any kind of relationship until I told my side of what happened. When I saw you, I saw her and I couldn't get past that, even though Erin kept telling me you weren't your mother." He cocked one side of his mouth. "Did I tell you I'm a stubborn man?"

She laughed. "Yes, but I figured that out on my own."

"I'm also blunt. Where do you and I stand?"

"You're my uncle and Erin's father. And to be blunt myself, it's easier to forgive you than my mother."

"I know. She had such potential, but she became friends with the wrong people who used her until she had nothing left. In the past years, I had been keeping tabs on you when Erin told me about meeting you at your mother's funeral. It didn't take me long to realize you aren't like my sister. You may look like her, but that's where the similarities stop."

She dipped her head. "Thank you. I worked hard not to be. If I learned anything from my mother, it was what I wouldn't do."

The chimes of the doorbell rang.

Her uncle looked toward the doorway. "I hope that isn't more people wanting to see how I'm doing."

"You mean, you don't love the attention?"

"Not one bit. I need the rest instead."

Selena spied Nicholas in the entrance with Brooke beside him. She smiled at Brooke. "It's nice to see you again."

"Hey, how about me?" Laughter danced in Nicholas's eyes.

"I already saw you earlier. Brooke, this is my uncle." She swung her attention to him. "She helped Nicholas protect me after the break-in. Mercy is her K-9."

Brooke crossed to Selena's uncle and shook his hand. "I brought the wig and a piece of clothing from Erin's house."

Her uncle's expression perked up. "To see if it was her the other night?"

Nicholas took the paper sack and removed two pieces of clothing—a blouse and a jacket. "Did Erin wear these much?"

"I know the jacket was her favorite. I don't know about the blouse," her uncle said.

"I got both of these from her hamper, so she had worn them before she went missing."

Selena stood and looked behind Nicholas. "Where's Max?"

"In the kitchen until I've hidden the wig, then I'll bring him in here to find it."

After Nicholas put the wig in a cabinet in the corner, he left and a moment later returned with Max. Selena held her breath as Nicholas took out the clothing and had his dog sniff it. She glanced at the anticipation on her uncle's face that mirrored how she felt. If Max didn't seek out the wig, then it wasn't Erin who'd been wearing it.

TWELVE

A band tightened about Selena's chest as she watched Max sniff the air then put his nose against the tiled porch floor and make a bee-line for the corner where the cabinet sat. He pawed the wooden door on the left side where Nicholas had stashed the wig. He moved to his K-9 and opened the cabinet. Max stuck his head in, sniffed then barked several times.

"Good boy." Nicholas gave his partner a treat and removed the wig. When he turned toward her, a grin spread across his face. "It has been confirmed. The person wearing this wig wore those clothes."

Relief flooded Selena. She twisted toward her uncle. "Erin is alive!"

He grinned. "Praise God." He sank against the back cushion on the love seat. "Now all we have to do is find her and prove she is innocent. She won't be safe until we do."

"I agree, Senator Eagleton. We aren't sure

who was the target when you were shot. It could have been Selena, but there's the possibility you were the intended victim to lure your daughter out of hiding. It almost worked." Nicholas handed the sack to Brooke.

After she left, Uncle Preston said, "I'd been wondering that, too. And if Selena was the target, it's probably because she's looking into those cases Michael was working on."

"All I know is that your niece's snooping has stirred up a hornet's nest."

Petting Max next to Nicholas, Selena chuckled. "I'm glad to oblige."

"So what's next?" her uncle asked, rising from the couch.

"We have a lead on an aide we've been looking for." Nicholas swung his attention from her uncle to her.

"Good. Please keep me apprised of the investigation into my shooting and Saul's murder, too."

"Yes, sir."

Uncle Preston walked slowly toward the doorway into the main part of the house. "Now to find some coffee and my newspapers to read. Work does not stop because I'm injured."

"I'd like Max to go with you, if that's all right, sir."

Her uncle glanced over his shoulder with a somber expression. "Just so long as he doesn't talk while I'm trying to read." A grin spread across his face.

When her uncle had disappeared from view, she laughed. "I know Max has many talents, but so far talking isn't one."

"Max thinks he does when he barks. It's good to see your uncle kidding."

"Yes. We had a good talk about my mother. I realized I could forgive Uncle Preston, but I still haven't been able to let go of my anger toward her. Do you think it's because I might be able to have a relationship with my uncle, but since my mother has died, I can't with her?"

"Do you think that's it?"

"Answering my question with one of your own isn't any help."

"Think about it. You were estranged from both of them and not because of anything you did." Nicholas stepped closer, clasping her hand. "So why are you still mad at your mom?"

"Because I can't talk to her and tell her how I feel. She's gone."

"But you can still tell her how you feel. Nothing is stopping you. Let it go."

"Have you let your past go?"

He tilted his head to the side. "I'm working on it."

"I guess I can say the same thing." She peeked around Nicholas. "Now that we're alone, were you referring to a lead on Janice Neill's whereabouts?"

"Yes. Isaac has left for a small town in Delaware to interview her."

"Why aren't you?"

"Because I'm not leaving you and your uncle. He'll call me as soon as he's finished the interview. We've hit a dead end with the other aides that went to Tabitha's the day Saul Rather and Greg Littleton got into that argument. Brooke told me when she arrived earlier that the stolen motorcycle I saw fleeing the Eagleton estate was found—at Tabitha's apartment's covered parking. It had been parked there for days. When the custodian who took Littleton's job realized it didn't belong to a tenant, he reported it to the police. We'd already talked to the owner earlier about it being stolen and ruled out the man for the shooting. I think someone is trying to frame Tabitha as well as Geary."

"Like the first one in the underground parking garage. Why a motorcycle not a car?"

"In a chase, they can go places a car can't. It does mean the shooter is a practiced motorcyclist since he or she feels comfortable using it as a getaway vehicle, so we've added that information to cross-check against the suspect list."

"Any word on the break-in of General Meyer's office?"

"We have a short list of suspects, but no concrete evidence to make an arrest."

"What's your gut feeling about who did it?"

"Vincent Geary. There's something about the man that doesn't feel right. And I could see him wanting intel on the Jeffries case."

"So you think he had something to do with Michael's death?"

Nicholas rubbed his chin. "Maybe, or he just wants to know all the latest for the congressman."

"But Congressman Jeffries would be filled in on the investigation."

"There are always pieces of information held back, even from a victim in the crime."

She set her fist on her waist. "So what are you holding back from me on my attacks?"

He smiled, his dimples appearing. "Nothing. I know better. Besides, you're the best one to help me with this, and I know you aren't involved in your attacks."

"You trust me?"

"Is there a reason I shouldn't?"

"No." The fact that Nicholas—who didn't trust easily—did trust her spread a warmth through her body.

He inched even closer. "So if you see or talk with Erin, you would tell me?"

"A few days ago I wasn't sure, but I am now. Yes, I would."

"What changed your mind?"

"You."

His arms slipped around her. "You trust me."

"Yes."

The softness in his eyes held her roped to him. She didn't want to move from his embrace. "Thank you." He dipped his head toward hers, paused and pulled back. He took a step away, releasing her. "You're a distraction. When this is over, I'm going to kiss you properly."

Although disappointed, she laughed. "I'm going to hold you to that."

Later that afternoon, Nicholas hung up from talking with Isaac and turned toward Selena sitting beside him on the couch. "We have a few more pieces of information to help us."

"What did Janice Neill say?"

"We have some more names of regulars at Tabitha's weekly get-togethers, and Janice is pretty sure most of them attended frequently that summer. Nancy Jackson, Carly Jones and Adele Carpenter."

"Nancy still works for Senator Langford, and Carly Jones and Adele Carpenter work for my uncle."

Nicholas smiled. "Also, Vincent Geary stopped

by a couple of times, as well as Adam Hansom, an aide for Congressman White. Both White and Langford were Vincent's alibi for the night of your attack in the parking garage."

"How is this going to help us? It's just more names to add to a list that seems to be growing." Selena massaged her temples.

"Are you all right?"

"I have a headache, but I'll be fine." Selena sighed. "So it seems we need to find out who rides a motorcycle."

"Exactly. Fiona will cross-check all these names with any history of biking."

"Maybe we're grasping at straws."

"Sometimes it's the little things that trip someone up."

"That'll be a lot of digging into a person's past."

"That's Fiona's expertise—getting information."

"Are you going to interview each one?"

"No, I'll send Brooke, except for Carly and Adele who work for your uncle. I'll ask him to request they come to the house."

"I'll give a call to the office and tell Carly that my uncle wants to see her and Adele."

"You think they'll come?"

"Why do you want to see Carly and Adele?" Senator Eagleton asked from the doorway into the den.

Nicholas told him about Tabitha's get-togethers after work and why he wanted to talk to both women.

Scowling, the senator took a chair across from Nicholas. "I'll do it if you'll let me know what they say. I don't understand why who was at Miss Miller's is important to the Littleton case."

Nicholas leaned forward and rested his elbows on his thighs. "A handful of people witnessed the big argument between Littleton and Rather, which became important in the trial because it gave Littleton a motive for killing Rather. We've checked out the ones who testified at the trial, but Littleton remembered looking up to Tabitha's balcony and seeing three women watching Rather accuse Littleton of stealing from him."

"Did Littleton rob Saul?"

"No, the real thief was caught a few months after Littleton's trial with a few of Rather's items in his possession. The man confessed but had an alibi for the time of Rather's murder."

"What about the couple who testified against Littleton?" the senator asked. "I remember their testimony, particularly the wife's, was damaging about how angry Littleton was when Saul accused him."

"I talked to Mr. Quincy," Leaning back, Nicholas stretched his legs out. "His wife was visiting her sister, but he told me that she had a tendency to exaggerate the facts."

Selena sat forward. "Why didn't he say anything at the time of the trial?"

"He was afraid she'd get in trouble."

Selena frowned. "Then why did he tell you that the fight between Littleton and Rather wasn't like what his wife had said?"

"Remorse. He felt Littleton was red with embarrassment, not anger, at the pool. It has been bothering him."

"What did Tabitha say when you interviewed her?" Selena took a composing breath.

"She remembered the fight but didn't pay a lot of attention to Littleton, only Rather."

"How about the other two ladies on the balcony?"

"She couldn't remember who else was there except Becky Wright, who couldn't give me much more than what Tabitha did."

Senator Eagleton picked up the phone on the end table and called his office.

Selena moved closer to Nicholas and whispered, "Michael made a note to talk with Mrs. Quincy after speaking with her husband. That was the day he died. Do you think he told Michael the same thing?"

"I'll call and ask Mr. Quincy. I have his number in my notes." Nicholas left the den as the senator wrapped up his conversation with Carly.

He retrieved what he needed and found a private place to make the call.

"Mr. Quincy, this is Officer Cole of the Capitol K-9 Unit. I have a question about what you told me about your wife's testimony."

"Just a minute. She's here, and I don't want her overhearing me."

Nicholas heard a sound like a door shutting.

"Okay. I'm outside and can talk. You do remember you promised me my wife wouldn't face any repercussions concerning her testimony."

"Yes. What I need to know is did you tell Michael Jeffries the same thing when he came to see you about your wife's exaggeration of what she saw?"

"It was just my opinion and I made that clear to Mr. Jeffries, but yes, I told him. He seemed excited by what I said. I wanted to tell the court I thought Greg Littleton wouldn't have stolen from anyone at the apartments. I never got the chance to say it. The DA cut me off."

He wasn't as familiar with the trial transcript as Selena, so he asked, "Did the defense ask you to elaborate about Littleton's character?"

"No."

"Thanks." Nicholas pocketed his cell phone and returned to the den.

"Carly and Adele are on their way," the senator said. "I'm going to run through some details for the party this weekend with Carly, so talk with Adele first. Neither lady has given me any reason to suspect them of this crime. Murder? That's hard for me to believe."

Nicholas sat next to Selena. "Tell me about Saul Rather. What kind of intern was he?"

"He was driven, very capable at his job and would have probably gone far in politics. When I interviewed him for the internship, he told me he hoped one day to run for office. The only drawback was that he was a ladies' man, and we've seen how that can get a politician in trouble."

"Did you ever see him with Tabitha Miller?" Nicholas asked.

Senator Eagleton firmed his lips and stared at the floor for a minute. "I think she came to the office one time not long before he was killed. I saw them when I left to go to the Capitol. They were arguing, or at least Tabitha wasn't happy with him." He tilted his head. "You know, I wouldn't have thought about that if you hadn't asked."

"Did he ever flirt with members of your staff?"

Selena's uncle grinned. "If she was a woman under forty, he flirted."

The sound of the doorbell filled the house.

Nicholas rose. "I'll send Carly in to see you while I talk with Adele."

When Nicholas came into the foyer, Max

stood waiting for him. His K-9 greeted every visitor. Nicholas opened the front door to allow Carly and Adele into the house. "Senator Eagleton will speak with you in the den, Ms. Jones, while I talk with you, Ms. Carpenter."

Adele stiffened. "Why?"

"I have a few questions concerning the Jeffries case." Out of the corner of his eye, he could see Carly lingering by the entrance into the den down the hall. He gestured toward the living room a few steps away.

Adele went ahead of him, shaking her head. "I don't know anything about that case. I never even met the congressman's son."

"I understand." He waved his arm toward a chair while he sat in the one across from her. "Have you ever attended a get-together at Tabitha Miller's after work?"

"Sure. I was a regular a couple of years ago, but lately I haven't. What's this got to do with Michael Jeffries's murder?"

"Two years ago in June, did you go to one?"

"I'm sure I did. I usually went with Carly once or twice a month back then."

"Were you there when an argument broke out between two men outside by the pool?"

Her forehead knitted. "Yeah, I heard one huge fight. I even went to the balcony and peeked out. Tabitha and Becky were watching. I really wouldn't call it an argument so much as Saul

Rather screaming at some man. I'd never seen Saul go off like that."

"What did the other man do?"

"He was totally uncomfortable. He kept looking around as though searching for a way to escape."

"Did that man say anything to Rather? Shout back?"

"He just said he wasn't the one, then tried to calm Saul down."

"Did the man look angry?"

Adele closed her eyes for a few seconds. "I don't think so and certainly not like Rather."

"Who else was at the get-together that day?"

"I can't remember specifically except Tabitha, Becky and Carly. Sometimes different people came and went. In fact, a couple of times before Saul was killed, he went to Tabitha's get-togethers but not that day."

"How did the argument end?"

"Saul finally just stormed off." Adele relaxed against the chair and crossed her legs.

"When you went back inside, did you all discuss the incident?"

"Yes. We often ended up talking about the latest gossip. Carly was surprised at Saul's anger, too, so he became the object of our conversation that day."

Nicholas rose and handed her a business card.

"If you remember anything else about that day, please contact me."

She pushed to her feet. "Saul's murderer was caught and convicted. Why the interest now?"

"I can't comment on an ongoing investigation."

Adele snapped her fingers. "You don't think the building janitor killed Saul."

"I didn't say that."

"You don't have to," Adele said, a satisfied expression on her face as she exited the living room.

When they entered the den, the senator finished up with his chief of staff. "So the security will be upgraded by Saturday?"

Carly nodded. "They've been working all week. I'll go out Friday and check it over with the supervisor of the project."

The senator looked at Nicholas. "Do you need to talk with Carly?"

"No, sir. I got what I needed from Ms. Carpenter."

Frowning, Carly glanced between her boss and Nicholas. "What did you need?"

"Some information about a fight between Saul Rather and Greg Littleton by the pool the night before Rather's murder. Ms. Carpenter told me she was the third person on the balcony watching the exchange." Nicholas observed Carly intently.

"Oh, I remember hearing about that fight. Adele told me Saul laid into the other man." Carly stood and turned toward her boss. "If that is all, Senator Eagleton, we need to return to the office."

Nicholas escorted both women to the door then locked it after they left. When he looked toward the den, Selena emerged and came toward him.

"Did she give you anything to help the case?" Selena asked.

"Possibly. She confirmed that Littleton wasn't really angry but uncomfortable by the scene Rather created. I'm beginning to see why Michael was interested in the case. Something doesn't feel right here."

"But you don't know what?"

"No, but if we can prove someone else had a better motive, that'll be a start. I'd like to go back and talk to Littleton, but I don't want to leave you."

She stepped closer, her scent wafting to him. "I'll be fine. This place is secure. You can even leave Max to protect me and Uncle Preston. Remember, I'm capable of taking care of myself. I brought my gun with me."

"I should have frisked you for weapons," he said with a chuckle. "I'll go to the prison on Friday and then check the security at the estate."

"You don't trust Carly's assessment?"

"You know I don't trust easily. I want to see it with my own eyes."

She pressed against him, smiling up at him. "But you trust me? Remember before you answer, I have my gun upstairs."

Laughing, he gave her a light kiss on the forehead. "I think you know the answer. You're at the heart of my investigation. Usually my only partner is Max."

She moved back. "I'll take that as a compliment."

On Friday, Selena met Carly in the hallway at her uncle's town house. Uncle Preston had asked Selena to let his chief of staff know he was on the back porch. After Selena did, she asked, "Had Nicholas arrived at the estate before you left?"

"No, was he supposed to? I thought he was staying here all the time."

"Usually, but he had to interview someone and decided to go look over the security on the way back."

"I'm surprised he didn't have the person he's interviewing meet him here like Adele and me."

"He couldn't in this case." Selena removed her cell phone from a pocket and headed down the hall. "I'll just call him and see where he is."

Selena went into the living room before punching in the numbers. With the sheers pulled closed, she stood at the window, a security guard with a dog making his rounds. When Nicholas answered, she asked, "What did Greg say? Anything new that might help us."

"Actually, yes. He remembers hearing the sound of a motorcycle when he walked toward the parking garage right before he found Saul's body. He didn't think too much about it because he figured the motorcycle was on the street. No one at the apartment complex had a bike."

"So a motorcycle shows up again, this time at the crime scene. Interesting. How's Fiona coming with the list of people at the White House who've ridden a bike?"

"Slowly, but she's diligently working on it. If the information is out there to find, she'll find it."

"How's Greg? Holding up?"

"He says he's okay, but I don't think so. I should be back soon. I'm finishing up at the estate. Everything seems all right, but I wish the senator would postpone this fund-raiser until the case is solved."

"Which one? Michael's or Saul's?"

"Both. See you in a little while."

As she disconnected with Nicholas, she thought she heard a sound in the foyer and turned. When she walked to the entrance into the living room and checked the entry hall, she didn't see anyone. Maybe it was Max or her imagination?

She hurried to the porch since her uncle had wanted her to be present as he and Carly were discussing tomorrow night's party.

"Oh, good. We can start now," her uncle said as she took a seat. "I was telling Carly that you'll be my hostess. Erin usually is, but..." His voice trailed off into silence as he looked away.

Surprised by the statement, Selena thought she might have heard wrong. "Hostess?"

He returned his gaze to her. "With all that's been happening, I've forgotten to ask. I hope you will."

"Well, sure. What do I need to do?"

"After we greet everyone who has shown up, I usually move around the room. When it's for the Eagleton Foundation, I actively solicit donations, but in this case there will be others doing it for the Wounded Heroes Organization, so we won't be the only ones."

"Good, because if I had to depend on working as a saleswoman, I'd probably starve," Selena said.

"Me, too," Carly added.

For the next hour they discussed the different aspects of the fund-raiser, from the food to the A-listers attending. When they had finished, Nicholas showed up in the doorway to the porch, Max beside him.

"Did I miss anything?" he said with a smile, his gaze finding Selena's.

"I'm playing hostess tomorrow," Selena said, a part of her uncomfortable taking Erin's place next to her father. "I'm going to be helping to get donations for Wounded Heroes. I'll need to read up on the charity so I can answer questions."

Nicholas winked at her. "I'll help. I'm a big supporter of the organization."

"Oh, great. You can be my first donor. Bring your checkbook tomorrow night."

Carly rose. "How did the security look at the estate?"

"Good. It will be hard for someone to get inside without being invited."

"I'm glad. That's what I thought." Carly turned to Selena's uncle. "I'll be waiting for you at the estate. See you all tomorrow afternoon."

As Nicholas escorted Carly to the front door, her uncle uncrossed his legs and sat forward. "You looked worried about something. I should have asked you to be my hostess in private. That way, you could have declined. I don't want you to do anything that'll make you uncomfortable."

"I'm fine. I'm used to big receptions. No, I was just thinking Erin should be here doing it."

A look of sadness captured her uncle's expression. "So do I."

Feeling as though she'd intruded on her uncle's grief, Selena peered away and caught sight of Nicholas returning. He believed in Greg's innocence. It wouldn't be long before she would convince him Erin was innocent, too. Selena sent him a smile. For all her independence, what would she have done without his help?

After changing into a royal blue cocktail dress and matching high heels she was wearing to the fund-raiser, Selena descended the stairs to the first floor at her uncle's mansion fifteen minutes before the guests were to arrive. Although Carly had probably already checked on the food, as the hostess, Selena felt it was her duty to make sure it was what her uncle wanted.

Handsome in a tuxedo, Nicholas stepped into the large foyer and stared at her as she came downstairs. She gripped the wooden banister to keep from falling because his intense gaze made her self-conscious. Her knees weakened. Dressed as he was, she realized how well he fit into this wealthy environment, whereas she'd had to overcome her nerves and keep repeating that she was good at her job.

With her gaze glued on him, Selena knew she had to put some distance between them. She was becoming too dependent on Nicholas. She looked forward to seeing him, to what he said. And when he wasn't around, she missed him. *I am not my mother. I don't need a man to complete me.*

At the bottom of the steps, Nicholas came up to her, letting his attention move down her length slowly before returning to her face. "You look beautiful."

Memories of her mother and various men paraded across her mind. She forced a smile and pushed the thoughts away, but she couldn't totally dismiss them. "Thank you. I needed that. I'm getting nervous. As the White House tour director, I'm usually behind the scenes and very comfortable with that."

"It's your turn to shine and believe me, you will."

Maybe she could request someone different than Nicholas to guard her and her uncle. Brooke wouldn't threaten her piece of mind. Scare her like Nicholas did. She started to say something, when his cell phone rang.

"It's Fiona. I've got to take this."

"That's fine. I'll be in the dining room."

Did she have any good news for them? Earlier, Fiona had made her way through almost three-fourths of the list that Nicholas had given her and, other than Vincent Geary, she couldn't find anyone who rode a motorcycle. She knew Vincent had an alibi for the evening she was attacked in the parking garage. How about the day her uncle was shot? She knew that Nicholas would check out his alibi for each occasion where a bike was used. But that didn't mean someone couldn't have hired a person to do the job. Vincent was on the top of Nicholas's list for breaking into the general's office, which made him a prime suspect in her eyes. And the most damaging piece of evidence against him was that he had lied to Nicholas about being able to ride a motorcycle.

She walked around the buffet layout in the dining room, stopping to make sure there was a serving spoon for the artichoke dip. After the party tonight, she could talk with Nicholas about someone else guarding her. Or better yet, she could persuade her uncle to request Brooke. Chicken. That wasn't like her, and that scared her even more.

She spied Nicholas coming toward her, his features set in grim lines. "What did Fiona find out?"

"Tabitha Miller used to ride a motorcycle in high school and even race off-road. I called Isaac to bring her in to headquarters and interview her."

"What about her alibi for Sunday when my uncle was shot?"

"What if someone else was in her car or she and Vincent Geary worked together. They both work for Congressman Jeffries. They could have known what Michael was working on." Nicholas glanced at his watch. "I'll have to worry about this later. Isaac will handle Tabitha. We need to get through this evening without any problems. It's showtime. Ready?"

"Yes, Uncle Preston is in the living room. I think the downstairs of my house is smaller than his living room."

"Perfect for these kinds of large parties but harder to keep an eye on the whole room at once." Nicholas offered her his arm and escorted her to her uncle, who stood next to Carly in the foyer just outside the living room.

Her uncle grinned at her. "Our first guests have arrived. I appreciate your being here."

"Good. Just remember that when I insist on you leaving the party before you wear yourself out."

Her uncle harrumphed.

"I owe it to Erin to take care of you."

Before he could say anything else, the first guests came into the foyer. For the next hour Selena met hundreds of people, some she knew from her job. Names swirled around in her mind, and she tried to keep everyone straight. Many of them knew Nicholas, and he ended up greeting people while he stood beside her.

As Carly left, her uncle turned toward her. "Now the fun part starts, persuading these guests to fork over money to a good cause."

"I don't think it will be too hard. They came to the fund-raiser."

"We need to split up." Her uncle headed toward a group of senators.

She looked at Nicholas. "I want you to stay

near him. If you think he's overdoing it, please let me know. I'm going to talk with General Meyer."

Nicholas watched her uncle across the room. "Not without me."

"Afraid of what I'll find out about you?"

His gaze zeroed in on her. "Yes," he said in dead seriousness. When he chuckled, his eyes sparkled. "No, I'm afraid of what you'll tell her."

Selena winked at him. "You should be."

For an hour she went from one group of guests to the next, pleased by the number of pledges she received for Wounded Heroes. Every once in a while she found her uncle and Nicholas in the crowd. Both were talking to the people around them. She enjoyed watching them.

When she moved into the dining room to make sure everything was flowing smoothly with the food, Congressman Jeffries approached her.

"I've heard about all the problems you've had lately," he said.

She didn't know what to reply. She knew of Nicholas's suspicions the congressman wasn't what he appeared to be, but everything she'd heard about him was good. "Nothing like what some wounded soldiers have when returning to the States. I hope you'll support a good cause," she chose to say rather than talk about the case.

He chuckled. "Preston has already hit me up,

but I have no problem giving more." He took out his checkbook and made another generous donation. When he gave the check to Selena, he smiled. "Your uncle and I might disagree on some issues, but I'm glad you're here to make his life easier."

When he left, Selena stared at his retreating back. She could see why the congressman was so popular.

"Ma'am, I have a note for you," a waitress said next to her.

She looked at the woman then took the note. "Who gave this to you?"

"A man in the living room."

"Thanks." As the waitress disappeared in the crowd, Selena read the message. *Meet me in the library. Good news. Nicholas.*

The handwriting looked similar to what little she had seen of his. Maybe the good news was about Isaac's interrogation of Tabitha Miller. This might be the best time to talk to him about Brooke taking over the protection detail. She headed back into the foyer, looked around for Nicholas, and when she didn't see him, started down the hallway to the library.

He wasn't there, either. She scanned the room again. She began to back into the hallway, when she felt a prick at her neck. Everything twirled before her eyes and darkness fell.

THIRTEEN

Nicholas panned the crowd in the dining room where he'd seen Selena heading fifteen minutes ago. When he didn't find her there, he glanced around the large foyer. Where was she? She wasn't in the living room. Maybe there had been a problem with the food, and she'd gone to the kitchen. As he made his way there, he asked a couple of security guards if they had seen her.

A guard near the hallway that led to the den, restrooms, office and library said, "She went down the hall about ten minutes ago."

"Do you know where?"

"She turned at end of the hall, which only leads to the library. Do you want me to look for her?"

"No, I will. Did anyone else go to the library?"

"No. Just Miss Barrow."

Maybe she needed quiet time. He could certainly understand that. Nicholas strode toward the library. When he went inside, he found an empty room and the window open. His gut clenched.

He hurried to the window and looked out. When he examined the sill, a royal blue swatch of fabric riveted his attention. Selena wouldn't leave without letting him know—at least willingly and especially out a window.

His blood iced. He needed Max.

He spun around and rushed into the hall, stopping at the end to talk to the guard again. "Are you sure no one else went to the library?"

"Yes, sir. I note where everyone goes when they walk past me. Right now one woman is in the restroom. That's all."

"Put out an alert that Selena Barrow is missing. I want everyone to be on the lookout for her."

Nicholas made his way to General Meyer near the dining room. "Ma'am, I think someone took Selena from the library. I'm going to track her from there and see what I find."

"I'll handle everything here. We're going to lock down the party and gather everyone into the living room."

"Because of all the precautions, if someone took Selena, it probably was one of the guests or staff."

"I know. I'll take care of this end."

As General Meyer gathered some of the security guards and began to corral the guests and servers into the main room, Nicholas pushed through the crowd and retrieved Max in the kitchen. He put a leash on the rottweiler then hurried upstairs to get an article of Selena's clothing. In the library, Max sniffed the blouse she'd worn earlier, found her scent by the door and followed it to the open window.

Not wanting to damage any evidence on the window, he hastened to the nearest exit and had Max pick up the trail outside below the window. His K-9 tracked Selena's scent to an empty spot in the parking area. One of the security protocols he'd put into effect before the guests arrived was for the guards to note who parked where.

Nicholas spied a guard with a clipboard and asked him, "Did you see this car leave?"

"No, sir. It was here about fifteen minutes ago."

"Who parked here?"

The guard checked his list. "Carly Jones."

"What was the license plate and make and model of the car?" He'd told the guards before everyone arrived to add that information down on their list.

The man gave him the information.

Nicholas placed a call to Fiona, who he hoped was still at headquarters. On the fifth ring she picked up.

"You must have been reading my mind. I

finished the last person on the list minutes ago and was going to call you."

"This is an emergency. I need you to send out a BOLO on this car and its driver, Carly Jones. I believe she's kidnapped Selena from the party. Tap into traffic cams in this area. I need to know where she is taking Selena."

"It's not like the city has traffic cams in a lot of places."

"I know. I need something to indicate where to find Selena. Anything." Desperation edged his voice, and he didn't bother to mask it. He had to find Selena unharmed. He'd never forgive himself if he didn't.

Selena slowly felt sensations—the feel of leather against her cheek, a musty smell that roiled her stomach and the sense of moving. Was she in a vehicle? She tried to move. She couldn't. Rope dug into her wrists, which were tied behind her back, and bound her ankles.

She inched her eyelids up. Darkness surrounded her, but she could tell she must be in some kind of SUV. Suddenly it went over an obstacle, and she bounced.

"Sorry about that. The road is getting a little rough."

Carly?

She decided not to say anything, but she continued to try to assess what was happening.

"Playing possum?" Her uncle's chief of staff cackled. "I know how long what I gave you would last. I want you to know what's going to happen to you since you've ruined my life. I've given your uncle the best years of my life and then you start snooping."

"What are you talking about?" Maybe playing clueless would get her some answers.

"Ah, so you are awake. We're almost there."

Where was *there*? Selena lifted her head to see what she could make out in the dim light from the dashboard. Another bump sent her to the left, and she hit her head against something she thought was—a stick—no, a handle.

With her arms behind her, she couldn't reach it to see what it felt like. She scooted and rocked until she managed to sit up on the backseat. "Where are we?" She needed information and the only one that had that was Carly.

"We're on I-95. Once I dispose of you, I'll make my escape. I have it all figured out, and if I can't escape, you're going to be my bargaining chip." Carly exited the highway. "But I don't think I'll have a problem. I've got a boat ready to take me wherever I want to go if I couldn't stop you from looking into Saul's death. Why didn't you leave it alone?"

"Did you kill Saul?"

"Duh. Yes. He tried to blackmail me. I wouldn't allow that. He should have known that. If I take bribes to sway the senator's point of view, then I wouldn't think twice about protecting my cash cow."

"Cash cow?"

"My job. Once I made chief of staff and became indispensable to the senator, I started planning ways to make money. There are a lot of lobbyists out there that have no problem paying for a vote, but with Senator Eagleton, that wasn't going to happen. One of the few men of integrity. So when I was paid off, I used any means I could to persuade the senator the way I needed. I worked hard for that money and no one was going to take it away from me."

"And that worked?" Selena tried to figure out where they were, but it was pitch-dark. From the headlights she glimpsed thick woods on both sides of the country road.

"About eighty percent of the time. Enough for me to stash a couple of million over a three-year span."

Selena squinted her eyes and kept her gaze trained on the landscape out the window. If she could manage to get away from Carly, she needed to know her whereabouts. "How did Saul find out?"

"He overheard an exchange with one of my best clients. He was going to blow the whistle on both of us if I didn't pay him." Carly pulled off the country highway onto an unpaved rougher road. "Even if they find this SUV, I'll be long gone by then."

"How? Walking?"

"Oh, no. I've got a motorcycle waiting for me."

"So you attacked me and shot my uncle?"

"Yes. No one asked me for an alibi. I had one for one of the times just in case. I took a lesson from Saul and blackmailed a client to provide it." Carly went off-road and parked. "Time for the next part of my plan." She exited the front seat and opened the back door nearest Selena. "I'm untying your feet, but don't try to get away. I have a gun and won't hesitate to use it, especially when I think of all the trouble you've caused me."

The interior light illuminated the weapon Carly stuffed in her pants' waistband. When had she changed? What time was it? "Where are we going?"

"To your grave."

"The SUV is stolen?" Nicholas asked Fiona on the other end of the phone call.

Everyone in the dining room quieted. The area had become the command center for the manhunt for Selena. The guests had left and law-enforcement officers were arriving. The senator had called in every favor he could think of to get as much help as possible.

"The vehicle doesn't belong to Carly Jones," Fiona said in a voice full of concern.

"But I've seen her driving it the past week."

"She stole it from one of her neighbors who is still on vacation to throw us off. I have a call in to them in Bermuda. The hotel said they went to dinner. They are checking to see if the couple is in one of their restaurants. As soon as I hear from them, I'll let you know. In the meantime, we are searching a ton of traffic-cam footage to see which way Carly went when she left the estate."

"Thanks. I know you are doing what you can. The general has computers being set up in here." When he hung up, he realized everyone was waiting for him to report what he'd discovered. "As you heard, the vehicle wasn't registered to Carly. It's her neighbors' SUV, and they are out of the country, so it hadn't been reported stolen."

"Can it be tracked?" General Meyer asked.

"Don't know. Fiona will find out. In the meantime, we look the old-fashioned way. I'm grateful for traffic cameras. They might be able to spot the car and track it."

Nicholas noticed the senator backing out of the dining room. His pallor concerned Nicholas. They were going to find Selena. He wouldn't rest until they did, but he didn't want her to return to find her uncle sick.

Margaret Meyer's gaze moved from Nicholas's to the senator's and back. "Go talk to him. This has got to be a reminder of when Erin disappeared. I have everything under control in here."

"But what if—"

"I'll let you know," the general interrupted, "if we find the car on one of the roads. In fact, we've got too many people on this. We're stumbling over each other." Then she turned away and went to speak with Dan Calvert and a few other Secret Service agents, who were there at the request of the president.

Nicholas found Selena's uncle in the living room, the furniture still arranged as it had been for the fund-raiser. He stood in front of the fireplace, staring at an empty grate as though a fire was blazing.

"Sir, are you all right?"

Senator Eagleton lifted his head and peered at Nicholas with eyes full of sorrow. "I can't go through this again. Erin is still missing. What if we never find her or Selena?"

Nicholas approached the older man, whose hands shook until he finally stuffed them in his pockets. "We will find both of them. I won't stop looking until we do. This time we know about the getaway vehicle and the person who took Selena. She only had a ten-or fifteen-minute head start before we started searching."

"I should have known Carly was capable of this. I trusted her with everything."

"And your knowledge of Carly can help us. Think about your conversations with her, especially in the last months. Is there a place she might go to hide? It could even belong to a friend."

The senator returned his gaze to the empty grate, his shoulders hunched forward. "I don't know. Maybe. I can't think." He glanced at Nicholas. "I've seen how you and Selena are. You care about her—she's more to you than just another assignment. How can you be so calm?"

"Because I have to be. I refuse to think we won't rescue her. The Lord is with her, protecting her until I can get there." In that second, he realized he loved Selena, and all he could do at the moment was put her in God's hands.

"But life doesn't work that way." The senator kneaded his nape. "What if…"

"Sir, I can't let worry take me down, or I won't be ready when I need to be." He laid his hand on the senator's shoulder. "Sit down and let's go through conversations you've had with Carly. How about the last vacation she took? Where did she go? What does she like?"

He thought a minute then replied, "The water. She always goes to the beach. In fact, a friend of hers has a boat."

"Do you remember where? Who she was talking about?"

"I don't know. I can't remember."

"Close your eyes and think back to when she told you about the boat."

Nicholas slipped into the chair across from Selena's uncle. There were so many marinas in Maryland and Virginia.

"It's not coming."

"Give it time. Relax. Don't force it." He'd used this technique many times in the past with witnesses. He prayed it would work this time. But he was struggling to keep his doubts from surfacing.

Lord, I need You. Give me peace to do what I need to do.

The general sat forward, snapping his fingers. "Virginia Beach."

"Okay. We can investigate the marinas…"

The general appeared in the entrance to the living room. "The SUV pulled off I-95 at Exit 152 near Prince William Forest. We think she's headed toward Highway 234."

"That's a big area." Nicholas rose. "But we can get the team down there and begin searching for the SUV. At least it's something to do and a start."

"Yes. I've called Gavin, and he's mobilizing the team."

Nicholas strode toward the foyer where Max

was. "We're on our way. I'll call Gavin, and maybe before I get there, Fiona will know if the vehicle can be tracked."

"I'm coming with you," the senator said as he stood.

Nicholas paused. "No, sir. I'm taking the helicopter that brought some of the White House Secret Service agents here. To put it bluntly, you'll slow Max and me down. I'll call you when I know something. Sir, see if you can remember the name of the person with the boat. Then we can locate the marina. If this is a dead end, we'll have that lead." At least Selena's uncle wouldn't be sitting around, waiting. He had something to do.

"I'll have a highway patrol officer meet you at the 152 exit." The general gestured for Nicholas to leave. "I'll keep you company, Preston."

Nicholas exited the house with Max, and in minutes he was in the air, heading for the national forest. He pictured the last time he'd seen Selena before she'd gone to the dining room. Their gazes had linked across the expanse of the living room. At that moment it had been tough to keep his professional facade in place. All he'd wanted to do was be alone with her.

In the dark forest, the only illumination Selena had was the flashlight Carly wore on her head. In one of Carly's hands she held her gun and in the other a shovel. Selena stumbled over something in the middle of a trail and went down on her knees. Without the use of her arms, which were tied behind her back, she barely caught herself from falling forward."

"Keep moving. We're almost there. Remember, if you try anything, I'll shoot you in the leg to keep you from escaping and then drag you to the spot I made for you."

Selena contemplated "trying anything." Maybe someone would hear the shot and investigate. That might be her only chance. The darkness could be used to her advantage. As she ran through one scenario after another, Carly grasped Selena's arm, causing her to stop, then shoved her into the underbrush on the side of the trail.

"This way. A couple of hundred yards and you'll meet your fate."

"The police will come after you. Why not run now? Leave me here. No one is around. I'm lost. I won't find help before you get away."

Carly laughed, a chilling sound in the cold air. "Sure. Do you want me to untie your hands first?" She used the handle of the shovel to poke her in the back. "Move!"

When Carly's light shone on a spot a few feet away, a small clearing, Selena knew they had arrived. In the middle there was a pile of dirt.

Another nudge with the shovel and Selena

came out of the thick forest. Carly illuminated the area. The sight of a hole in the ground about the size of a body sent a wave of panic through Selena.

As Nicholas climbed from the helicopter near where a highway-patrol officer waited at Exit 152 off I-95, his cell phone rang. Seeing who was calling, he quickly answered it. "Did you find anything, Fiona? I'm almost at the forest."

"Yes. The neighbor called me back and gave me the information to track his SUV. They had a tracking device put on it when they bought it."

"And?"

"I know where the car is parked right now. Off Highway 234 on an unpaved road, not for public use. I've got a forest ranger heading there to open the gates in case they aren't. You'll probably be there before him. I imagine Carly somehow opened them because the SUV isn't far past the second gate."

"Thanks. Let the captain know, so whoever is already here can head toward the area. Max and I will track them from the SUV." *Unless they're in the vehicle.* That thought made him rethink what he should do. "How far from the second gate?"

"It's hard to tell exactly, but not far."

He shook hands with the highway-patrol

officer and climbed into the front seat with Max in the back.

"Nicholas, you'll pass an RV campground," Fiona continued. "The turnoff is about a half a mile farther on your left."

"I'll let you know what I find." Nicholas ended his call with Fiona and relayed the information to the highway-patrol officer.

"I know that road. It's Spriggs Fire Lane," the Virginia state trooper said and pulled onto Highway 234. "It's not too far."

Fifteen minutes later, wearing night-vision goggles, Nicholas exited the patrol car, put Max on his leash and walked through the second open gate, leaving the officer to coordinate the others who would arrive shortly. He spied the SUV off the road. Gun in hand, he approached the dark vehicle and searched it to make sure Carly or Selena weren't around. Empty. He wasn't sure if he was relieved or not.

"Your turn, Max." Nicholas gave his dog the blouse to smell. "Find Selena."

Selena stared into the hole at a coffin.

"Get in it. I'm giving you a chance to be saved if they get to you before the air runs out. You're my bargaining chip." Carly waved the gun at Selena. She stared at the woman, realizing that she wouldn't see Nicholas again. She cared for him more than she ever had another. These emotions stirring in her were so different than anything she'd ever experienced. She wanted to explore them more in depth.

"I said, get in the coffin. Now."

"No."

"That isn't a choice." Carly charged Selena so fast it took her by surprise.

Carly contacted with Selena and sent her flying down into the pit. Her head hit against the side of the coffin and her sight blurred. Before she could scramble from it, the top slammed down while the darkness spun. A loud thump struck the wooden casket as if Carly had jumped down on top of it. Quickly, Carly hammered against the lid to keep it shut, causing shock waves of sound to thunder through Selena's mind.

I can't lose consciousness. Please, Lord, help me. Somehow.

FOURTEEN

A crashing sound echoed through the trees up ahead. Max kept going forward through the thick vegetation. Nicholas tried to speculate what the noise was, but he finally pushed it away and focused instead on getting to Selena before she was killed.

Through the eerie green of his view, he saw Carly jump into a hole. He increased his pace as much as he could without making noise. He needed to surprise the woman and prayed Selena was alive in the hole, the length of a grave. A pounding sound reverberated through the air. A few yards ahead of him, Max flew out of the underbrush toward Carly, her head visible above the ground.

"Get her," Nicholas shouted, lifting his gun.

Carly screamed.

When Nicholas planted himself at the edge of the grave, his weapon aimed downward, he found Max's mouth clamped around Carly's arm with the revolver. She lay on a coffin, a hammer by her feet.

"Get him off me."

"As soon as you let go of the gun."

Carly complied, and the weapon fell between the coffin and the dirt wall. Max was between Carly and the gun.

"Max, loose it. I've got her, boy." His K-9 partner dropped Carly's arm. "Where is Selena?" he demanded of Carly. "In the coffin?"

Flat on her back, Carly glared at him.

"Find Selena, Max."

His rottweiler scratched at the coffin at the same time Nicholas heard banging from beneath Carly. "I'm in here. Help."

"I'm here, Selena. I'll get you out." Then to Carly he said, "Climb out and lie facedown on the ground. One wrong move and I'll sic Max on you with no regrets."

Carly followed his order. As soon as the woman was lying on the ground, he pulled out his handcuffs and secured her.

"Guard her," Nicholas said then lowered himself into the hole, took the hammer and pulled the nails out of the wood.

When he lifted the lid, Selena launched herself into his arms, shaking against him.

He had so many things to say to her, but that would have to wait until Carly was taken care of.

He gave her a quick kiss then climbed from the hole and turned to help Selena out of her grave.

He stared into her beautiful features. "How are you?"

"I have one killer headache. Carly pushed me in and I hit my head, but that's nothing now. You saved me."

"I was only doing my job." He took out his cell and couldn't get reception. "We need to walk back to the Tahoe. There's a highway-patrol officer with a radio. You need medical attention."

"I'm fine. Really. And the best part is, I know why Carly killed Saul Rather. Greg will be freed soon."

The prison door opened, and Greg Littleton appeared in the exit. He looked around, saw Selena and Nicholas and waved. Bag in hand, the freed man hurried toward her and Nicholas. The sight of Greg's smile made her heart sing.

Selena watched as Greg cut the distance between them. "I can't believe this day is finally here. This is the best feeling."

"I agree," Nicholas said.

Greg stopped in front of Selena with a huge grin on his face. "I'll never be able to thank you two enough for what you did for me. I tried to convince everyone I was innocent, but no one would listen." He took Selena's hand. "Until Mr. Jeffries, then you."

Selena gave Greg a hug. "I'm so glad the truth finally came out."

"How did you two solve the case? I've heard some of it on the news." Greg swung his attention from Selena to Nicholas.

"It was mostly Selena. She got Carly Jones to tell her why she killed Saul Rather."

Greg's forehead furrowed. "Why would the woman confess to you?"

"Because she was going to kill me and she wanted me to know why." Selena glanced at Nicholas. "But he saved me." In the coffin, as Carly had hammered it shut, all Selena could do was pray and give in to the Lord. She wasn't going to get out of her situation without help, and Nicholas was the help the Lord had sent her. *Thank You, God*.

"As Senator Eagleton's chief of staff, Carly had been accepting bribes for several years and Saul found out," Nicholas explained to Greg. "He was blackmailing her, so she killed him. When she heard about the argument the evening before between you and Saul, she used that to frame you. Saul was meeting her for his first payoff, instead she shot him and fled as you came into the parking garage." Nicholas smiled at Selena. "She wouldn't stop digging deeper even when

Carly came after her at the Easter Egg Roll and in the White House underground parking."

"She was desperate toward the end and tried to shoot me at my uncle's. Instead, he was wounded. That's when Carly decided to leave the country with the money she'd accrued from the bribes she had taken."

"But she went after you first?"

"Yes, she wanted me to pay for ruining her scheme."

Nicholas clasped Selena's hand. "Can we give you a ride, Greg?"

Greg panned the area. "Thanks, but my mom should be here. We're going out to celebrate." His face lit up. "Ah, I see her coming."

"Greg, my uncle would like you to come visit him. He wants to offer you a job at his estate as groundskeeper."

"You're not joking?" Greg asked in a stunned voice.

"No." Selena gave him a piece of paper. "Call that number when you're ready."

"Thank you. Tell him I will." Greg shook Selena's hand then Nicholas's, then headed for the nearby Chevy and hugged an older woman waiting by the car.

Selena's throat clogged, and she swallowed several times before saying, "I'm glad I could finish what Michael started with the case."

"Come on. I've got one more place to go." He tugged her toward his Tahoe.

"Where?"

"A surprise."

As Nicholas headed toward Maryland, Selena relaxed, thinking about the whirlwind past few days since Carly had been arrested for Saul Rather's murder. "At least we found one murderer. I'd hoped Carly had killed Michael, too, then Erin could come home."

"Carly had an airtight alibi with a dozen senators able to verify her presence at a small party your uncle had given."

"And she was there the whole time?"

"Yes. Believe me, I went through her alibi, wanting to tear it apart. I couldn't. Neither could Isaac or Gavin."

Selena sighed. "Which leaves Erin where she was—a suspect."

"I'm not going to rest until the truth comes out. But I need you to promise to stop doing your own investigation. I can't go through the past few weeks again." Nicholas pulled up to a gate and pushed a remote control.

The black iron gates slowly opened. "I thought we were going to my uncle's."

"No, I told you I would bring you to my childhood home and that's what I'm doing."

Selena sat forward, looking out the windshield at the white-brick mansion with a long veranda across the front of the house and tall, massive columns. At least four chimneys thrust up toward the sky.

"This isn't that far from my uncle's."

Nicholas parked on a circular driveway near the massive double doors that led inside. "Actually, this place is closer than I realized. Probably no more than twenty minutes away." He opened his door and climbed from the Tahoe. "I want to show you the place."

She slid from the car as Nicholas rounded the hood. Was this his way of saying goodbye because neither she nor her uncle needed to be guarded anymore? The physical threat was over, and now she faced a different kind of threat. When she was praying to the Lord to be saved from Carly, she'd realized how she really felt concerning Nicholas.

"Why do you want me to see this?" she finally asked Nicholas, who paused and stared up at the front of the house.

A neutral expression descended, as if he was struggling to hide any emotion. "Because I needed to let my past go in order to move forward."

Move forward? Where? Doubts assailed Selena. "Have you forgiven your parents?"

"Yes. I can't change what happened, but I can put it behind me once and for all. I'm going to sell the place. This isn't me, but it will be perfect for someone else. I want some family to enjoy it the way it was meant to be enjoyed."

Her heartbeat thumped against her chest. "So you don't see you having a family one day?"

He shifted toward her and clasped her arms. "On the contrary, for the first time I do see me having a family—with you. That is, if you'll have me."

For a moment no words came, as if his declaration had robbed her of coherent thoughts.

"I know we haven't been together long, but I hope you'll give me a chance." Concern lined his face.

She flung her arms around him, pressing her body against his. "Yes. It's not the quantity of time we've been together that is important, but the quality of time. I know I should be scared of my love for you, but I've realized I'm not. You understand me."

He framed her face with his hands and peered down at her. "And you understand me."

"For years I was determined never to be like my mother. She had to have a man around. If she didn't, she couldn't function. I know I'm not ever going to be like her because I have for years lived a happy, content life." She looked into his beautiful eyes, full of love. "But you've changed that. If I went back to the way things were before I got to know you, I wouldn't be happy and content as before without you. There was a time

I would have been scared about that. I'm not now. When I needed someone, God sent you."

He leaned down and touched his lips to hers. "I love you, Selena." Then he deepened the connection, his arms entwining her.

The feeling of forgiveness toward her mother and of finally being free of her past spread through Selena as she poured all her love into the kiss.

* * * * *

If you liked this CAPITOL K-9 UNIT *novel,
watch for the next book in the series,
DETECTING DANGER by Valerie Hansen*

And don't miss a single story in the
CAPITOL K-9 UNIT *miniseries:*

Dear Reader,

It is always a pleasure to work with the wonderful authors who were a part of this continuity series. And an added bonus was dealing with police dogs. They are amazing at what they do.

I love hearing from readers. You can contact me at margaretdaley@gmail.com or at PO Box 2074, Tulsa, OK 74101. You can also learn more about my books at www.margaretdaley.com. I have a newsletter that you can sign up for on my website.

Best wishes,

Margaret Daley

LARGER-PRINT BOOKS!

GET 2 FREE LARGER-PRINT NOVELS PLUS 2 FREE MYSTERY GIFTS

Love Inspired®

Larger-print novels are now available...